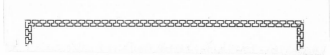

COMING ATTRACTIONS

Edited by Maggie Helwig & Bronwen Wallace

89

Acknowledgements: "The Blue Jacket" was previously published in *The Point.* "Contiguous" first appeared in *University of Windsor Review* and "Singing in the Dark" was originally published in *A Room of One's Own.*

ISBN 0 88750 767 0 (hardcover)
ISBN 0 88750 768 9 (softcover)

Cover art by John LaFarge
Book design by Michael Macklem

Printed in Canada

PUBLISHED IN CANADA BY OBERON PRESS

Introduction

This year's edition of *Coming Attractions* is one we're particularly happy with, featuring as it does three new writers who are already both accomplished and exciting.

Brian Burke is a Vancouver native, and a teaching assistant at Simon Fraser University. "I find it wiser for me not to say anything about my own work," he says. "I don't read them when they're finished." His stories here deal in one way or another with the disintegration of the family and even of the individuals within it. Tense, funny and bitter, they still offer some sort of reassurance—at least there are ties to be found, frayed and torn though they may be.

Michelle Heinemann lives in Calgary. Her work, haunted, disconnected and full of disturbing mysteries, is the most anxious and in some ways the most memorable in the collection.

Jean Rysstad lives in Vancouver, but grew up in Kintail, Ontario. The three stories included here—two of them part of a collection in progress—are the most "conventional" in narrative technique in this book. They are also the most rooted, the most sure of some sort of—if we must use the word—redemption. The couple in "Contiguous" remain "close, but not touching"; but the image we have chosen to end this *Coming Attractions* with—the mother and daughter on the long ride back to the coast, smelly with the little girl's vomit but still in each other's arms and "nearly home"—is an image of hope.

MAGGIE HELWIG

BRIAN BURKE

You Must Remember This

Shawn climbs the narrow rope of gravel laneway separating his father's house from his brother's, rising above him on the other side. Below him the long yard descends in tiers cut into the unstable slope. The small house sits at the bottom. They had all once lived there together, Shawn thinks to himself as he stands bareheaded in the rain, but now William lives across the lane and no-one knows where his sister Lesley is.

Every winter, heavy rains wash the top-soil into his father's low-ceilinged basement, and each spring another truckload is dumped onto the exposed garden. He grows salad crops, as Shawn calls them: lettuce, carrots, radishes, green onions and tomato plants in muddy balsa baskets.

William had simply levelled out a flat shelf of land and built high—high enough to overlook every other house in the area.

"Moved all the way across the lane, did he," Shawn said when he learned from his father that William had bought the old woodframe house and had spent the last six years on its reconstruction.

Shortly after that conversation, William called with the formal invitation. "Little brother," he crowed into the phone. "This is the first time you've lived in one place long enough to get your name in the phone book." Shawn had been living back east when William married. He had two nephews and a niece now.

His brother described the menu to him: hot slices of white and dark turkey meat, slabs of moist pink ham, green peas and carrots from the garden, and cranberry sauce. What William referred to as "plenty." Next it would be "bounty," Shawn thought. He could picture their best china and silverware on the table. A side dish of rice fried with bacon, mushrooms and soy. Candied yams as a special treat—their father's favourite. Shawn hated yams and he'd never known William to eat them. Eric, their father, ate yams. He liked to pile the empty skins by his plate.

"It'll be the whole family," William told him. "Susan's too. About time don't you think? The kids are curious about their Uncle Shawn. And there's lots of food. That should sound good to the proverbial starving student. I mean that as a joke. You know that."

"Yes. If I starve before the big event inject some turkey into my veins just in case it brings me around. 'Tis the season of births and rebirths."

"Then you'll come?"

Shawn had planned to spend Christmas with a girlfriend, but then she too received an invitation to return home. What was it about this time of year that drove families to seek reunion? For years he'd kept to his policy of not going out with anyone whose parents weren't dead. This woman's estrangement appeared to be as permanent as death. More miracles, Shawn decided. There was just no telling, this time of year. She'd been quite clear about not inviting him to join her.

"What? Not meet the folks on Christmas Day?" he'd said. "Good tax-paying alcoholics and child abusers, according to you?" He knew it was over for them. No surprise. He'd warned her: don't go back.

He spent Christmas Eve not exactly eager for trouble, after their fight, but looking for the thrill of having narrowly avoided trouble. He woke up this morning hung over and in time for another American bowl game on TV.

Shawn warms his hands in his coat pockets by clenching and unclenching his fists. He notices several small bikes lying in the rain, abandoned on his brother's uncut lawn. Condensation fogs the large panes of glass above William's balcony.

Shawn can't see inside. But in the loft above the living-room, he can see his brother hunched over in the sparse light of a lowered desk lamp. Bible hour. Preparation for a lesson at the Hall, to be delivered later that night.

He hasn't seen his brother since moving east to begin university, before William married and eight months after his sister Lesley disappeared for the second time. Born second and carefully balancing the division of the sexes, she had been the perfect buffer between two brothers.

He hesitates before the arched front door William rescued from scrap and renewed to varnished respectability. He waits for the light to switch on over his father's back door. His father will be watching television. Wrestling, Shawn guessed. Did they show wrestling at Christmas?

"Let me just say this, Bernie, I'm going to crush this guy's throat and let me wish you and yours all the best of the holiday season."

His mother, May, probably still fussed in front of her bedroom mirror, wondering if her red dress still suited her. Or maybe she was wrapping three more small surprises for her grandchildren.

Shawn also knows that his father, in his own brief bid for martyrdom, will refuse to pour himself a drink. The Hall, William's private church, condemns the use of alcohol.

"You mean externally, right?" Shawn had said, hearing the sad tone of his father's voice. Eric spent his week handing out turkeys and food hampers to the welfare recipients he called his clients. Occasionally, more than occasionally, accepting a drink bought with a welfare cheque he had issued and endorsed.

The light over the back door flickers on, releasing Shawn who knocks roughly at the door.

"Shawn—I saw you coming up the back alley," William shouts from his loft. "What took you so long? Checking the address?"

Shawn tosses miniature candy-canes to his brother's shy

kids. He's been carrying them with him all week, since the end of classes, giving them to professors, students, bus drivers.

"Get Susan to pour you something," William calls down. "There's a bit of everything."

"I'll be damned if there's a bit of anything," Shawn whispers to his eldest nephew. He wonders if he should have smuggled in a bottle. Like his father, he was clean. Relatively. Just two hits, earlier.

"Don't mind the kids. They're all wound up."

His two nephews and his niece regard him as if he were part pirate, part hobo. And maybe part serial killer too— God only knows what William's told them, he thinks with a smile.

"You must be the troops," he says.

"There's a present for you under our tree." This must be Jon, born before William's conversion.

"It's baby Jesus' birthday," his niece says, her child-smooth face solemn yet shining.

Shawn decides to sing for them. "Happy birthday to you, happy birthday to you, happy birthday dear Jesus, happy birthday to you." The girl, Michelle, claps. The youngest, Paul, merely stares.

"Did you know," Shawn says, "that Jesus is almost two thousand years old?" Michelle nods her head for him. "Now, about this present. Is it a big one or a little one?"

"It's pretty big," Jon says.

"Crawl under the tree and get it, then. We'll open it together. Talk to me after dinner," he says bending closer and lowering his voice. "I've got more candy-canes in my pockets."

Here it comes again, Shawn thinks when his parents arrive. All the excitement, every gift described without the taking of a second breath. His mother produces three more parcels. His lap is already piled high with GI Joe and his accessories.

Why not, Shawn thinks as he checks through their loot: kill a Commie for Christ.

"Merry merry," William says, descending from his loft. The rush of cold air from outside seems to sting his perpetually flushed face.

"Come in, come in and look at all this stuff. They made quite a haul. Hello again, Shawn. I see you've got yours."

Shawn unfolds the small religious pamphlet tucked inside the wrapping-paper of his gift. "Will You be Among God's Harvested Souls?" The accompanying sketch features a grim and then an even grimmer reaper. He decides he's supposed to opt for the merely grim one. Both carry scythes and look more like axe murderers than agents for the Lord.

"Thanks, troops," he says. "I can use the sweater. No heat in the residence."

"What's a residence?" Jon asks.

"It's a lot like a prison," Shawn says.

Michelle starts crying. "Uncle Shawn lives in jail," she says. She runs to her mother. All the kids look like her, Susan.

"I think your Uncle Shawn likes to tease," Susan says.

"None of us is wanted for anything serious," Shawn tells them. "The worst thing we do is grow things, just like Grandpa does."

Eric sits in the first chair he comes to. Shawn notices his new teeth and is distracted by the ill fit, the exposed slice of white enamel.

"Can I get you something, Dad?" William calls, this time from the kitchen. "I've got cola, orange, ginger ale, fruit punch, lemon lime, root beer." Shawn can hear him shifting the tins around in the fridge.

"Any of those." Eric uncrosses and recrosses his legs. He likes to sit with his legs up, on a recliner or a hassock.

"Ice?"

"Yes, ice. Lots of ice."

"Have you got your keys?" Shawn asks his Dad.

"In my coat pocket. Better ask your mother if she forgot anything before you go down. Small appliances, stocks, prime real estate."

"I didn't forget anything," May says from the kitchen. Everyone seems to have followed her in there. Shawn and his father are alone by the tree.

"Dinner soon," Susan tells him.

Shawn hurries down the path and across the lane. The down in his ski jacket has settled and thinned badly. A chill wind cuts him. He peers over his shoulder. Behind him, his brother's house, lit up, bustles with people passing by the windows, moving from room to room. Susan's parents must have arrived.

He trudges past his father's winter garden. No snow this year, just a settled dampness, and the garden eroding in a steady rain.

Inside, Shawn flicks on the toggle switch. He takes a bottle of his father's rye from the pantry, reads the label and twists off the plastic top.

"You'd think he could afford a better brand, now that there's just the two of them," he says aloud, his voice sounding familiar to him in the small house, as if this were his true voice and all the other voices he's spoken with for six years and more are inventions.

He fills a glass with ice and pours rye over the cubes as they crack. He'll give Susan's parents ten more mintes to spoil their grandchildren.

But then Shawn pours more, gives them another five minutes to exchange adult rounds of season's greetings—or seasoned green things as he proclaimed one year while handing out quarter-baggies of dry marijuana to his friends.

The perspiration on William's upper lip gleams as he sits at the head of the table. He's waiting for everyone to be seated before he begins grace. Shawn is laughing at Susan's father, who has come to the table with his nose scotch-taped to one side, broken so many times all the cartilage has been removed. Now it's Paul's turn to cry.

"Our Father we thank thee for the bounty of this meal and for the opportunity to come together as a family to share this feast, and for the love of our saviour Jesus Christ who died on the cross in agony for our sins, amen."

The children mutter amen. Susan and Shawn's mother say amen. Susan's father shows Paul how his nose works. He flattens it, takes Paul's finger and touches it to the nose-tip.

"I don't know about you guys," Shawn says, still aglow with rye, "but that sure lifted my spirits."

William brings out a new tape-recorder after dinner.

"The dishes can wait," he says, herding his wife back to the table. His wife, his mother and his mother-in-law. "Leave the dishes, leave the dishes."

William snaps on the machine. "I've got tapes here of the kids singing at the Hall," he says.

"We sang 'Jesus Loves Me,' Grandma. Jesus loves me this I know, for the bible tells me so—"

"This isn't me yet," William says.

"Do you sing too?" Shawn asks. "I'm not sure I'm ready for that."

"We all speak freely for about twenty minutes. We take turns with the lesson."

"Twenty minutes? How many have you guys gone forth and multiplied into?"

Jon still wants to sing. "Jesus loves me this I know..." but his mother holds his shoulders and places a finger on his lips.

Shawn leans back in his chair. He's had too much to eat and he'd like to undo the top button of his jeans. Paul plays in his bowl, squeezing the food between his fingers. Heat from the oven has melted the butter in the dish by Shawn's elbow and all that remains is a hardening yellow pool. Bits of turkey and green peas lie scattered across the red Santas and strange blue wreaths decorating the paper table-cloth. He watches as the last lazy fly of the year wrestles with a grain of fried rice.

"He got most of that from 'The Late Great Planet Earth,'" William says, gesturing toward the tape-recorder.

Shawn begins to sing. "You better watch out, you better not cry, you better not pout, I'm telling you why."

"Shawn..." his father warns.

"A much misunderstood song," Shawn says, cutting him off. "It postulates, in a metaphorical way, the possibility of an endless series of second comings. All of them without benefit of an armageddon. William? How does your theological training...hmmm, *theo* and *logical,* now there's an interesting combination...How does your training account for this?"

"The Bible's quite clear on that point. There is a definite need for Armageddon."

Should have brought that bottle, Shawn thinks. Or a joint. Could have pulled it out, taken a swig, passed it around the table. Voices, some clear, some rapturous, continue to speak. Shawn envisions tongues unravelling with the tape.

"Why are you so pissed off all the time?" his father asks.

Shawn picks soggy grains of rice from around his plate and brushes them off his fingers into his milk, notices his father's yam skins.

"You can't keep making fun of everything," William says. "Cynicism is faithless. There are things of value in this world."

Shawn leans across the table, closer to his two nephews and his niece. He opens his eyes wide, tilts his head at his brother. "He's right you know," he says with a smile.

"Your Uncle Shawn is always playing games," his mother says. She turns to Susan's parents. "He's always playing games. He is."

15

Shawn can sense this reassuring them, can see it slowly bringing half smiles to the children's faces. Susan's parents too. Everyone understands what games are.

2

He pushes himself back from the table and stands. "I need something down at the house," he says. "You want to give me a hand, Dad?"

"I gave you the key already."

"We won't be long. I'll get your coat." He doesn't blame Susan's parents for looking confused. They seem decent.

Shawn stares directly at his father. "You didn't want any more, did you?" he asks, nodding at the turkey carcass.

Outside, Shawn stretches his arms over his head and listens to the joints in his back and neck crack. "Sounds like they're going to play the entire service," he says.

"The kids' singing doesn't come until later."

"What's with all these stripped-down bikes? I feel like I'm in the bicycle graveyard. Is this where they all come to die?"

"He didn't have to invite us all, you know."

"But then he didn't, did he?"

Eric moves on in front, slipping and sliding down the backyard. Shawn searches for stars overhead, but none show through tonight. The air is still damp, cool enough to make him shiver but still too warm for this time of year. It doesn't seem right.

"You've heard his tapes before?"

"Couple of times. When he comes in from the Hall."

"Have you been?"

"Your mother went a couple of times."

Eric uses the handrail on the stairs down to his yard. He'd done the landscaping himself, each year adding stone walls, filling in the trenches behind the new masonry with junk and household garbage.

In the kitchen Shawn rips the ice tray from the unfrosted freezer, spilling water from the one he used earlier. He snaps it open with a sharp crack. His father prefers only a splash of cold water with his rye so Shawn mixes both drinks the same.

A reproduction of da Vinci's "Last Supper"—Judas clutching his sack of incriminating silver pieces, one apostle pointing while others appear shocked, questioning, argumentative about what's happened. Eric bought the picture for William and Susan's anniversary but they had refused to accept it. The Hall forbid idols of Christ. So it hangs in Eric's kitchen, the colours too bright, the frame part lamination and bits of mirrored glass. He gave William cash instead.

"Here's an idol the Hall does understand," he'd said, tossing William an orange and red $50 bill.

Shawn stirs their drinks with his finger and carries them into the living-room. He turns off the pole lamp and plugs in the tree.

"Thought you didn't drink rye." Eric raises his glass in a salute.

"Merry merry," Shawn says, "to quote your number one son. Thought you didn't like trees."

"Your mother likes to have one up."

Shawn holds his glass up to one of the yellow lights hanging from an upper bough. "William seems happy."

"That boy doesn't have to die to go to heaven. He's there now."

A blue light dangles loose at the front of the tree. Shawn places his glass beside it, stares through at the blue reflections. "Remember that time we took an axe up into the woods behind the gravel pit, looking for our own tree? 'Dad and Willie took an axe to cut down trees with Christmas whacks.' No snow that winter, either, and we kept complaining that it didn't seem like Christmas...hell, when *was* that Christmas that felt like Christmas?"

"Never did find a tree you both liked. Had to buy one anyway." Shawn had been relieved but couldn't tell his father, who had carried the heavy double-bitted axe over his shoulder.

"Can't figure out what got into him," Eric says. "He went first. Susan didn't care for it. She followed eventually though."

"What choice did she have? It was probably join or jump."

Eric tilts back his recliner. "She told me she went drinking one night while he was out saving souls. Says she poked around the bar a bit, listened to her girlfriends jabbering away. Decided the bar was hell. I told her, 'Not such a bad place to be, was it?' I guess it was, though, because she joined him. Claimed she belonged with the Jesus creatures. Her people weren't too happy. Nothing I could do."

"He's in good company. Lots of people being reborn, as if once wasn't enough. Especially after they've been arrested for something. Bob Dylan even became one. Got baptized in Pat Boone's pool. Not what John the Baptist had in mind way back when, I bet. When he still had his mind, or his head at least."

Shawn swallows a long drink, catching the ice on his upper lip, and he sits on the couch.

"Your mother left your Dylan posters on the wall in your room," Eric says. "That crazy one with all the colours? Still there. Along with the others."

"Came inside an album. Greatest Hits Volume One."

"I'm not sure William wants to share Christ with the likes of Bob Dylan," Eric says.

"It'll have to be Bob Dylan BC now. Before Christ. I don't like his new stuff."

Eric watches the ice slide down the inside of his glass as he lowers it to his lap. "I never know what to get them," he says. "You buy them anything?"

Shawn swallows rye and shakes his head. He's not normally a rye drinker. "No money."

"Your mother would have appreciated a card, probably."

"I never send any. They're a fraud."

"You should have got one. She likes to read cards."

Shawn wonders if there is any mix, something to dilute the strong taste. "Maybe William's right about this. He's uncanny that way. That's what's so frightening."

"Nothing scary about it. He's your brother."

"Oh, right."

"He loves you, in a Christian way, so he says."

"He loves mondo-God. As an afterthought that might include me but I'd prefer something a bit more specific, a bit more personal. I'm funny that way. I suppose his room's still the way it was?"

"The same. You mother cleans every day."

Shawn laughs. "All those glossy pictures of European soccer players no-one's ever heard of. In a country full of hockey, football and baseball. He always said that soccer was a purer sport. It just seems that way because poor people can play it. All you need is feet. That's why it'll never catch on over here. No equipment. How can a sport succeed in North America with virtually no equipment? No technology? No inflatable helmets to become faddish about? Nothing to trivialize. A sport with little promise of technology will never be popular here. No sizzle to sell."

Eric's head seems to block out the rest of the room, except for the tree in the corner. Shawn believes the name Eric should belong to a lighter man, a more athletic type.

"No Billy Graham posters on his walls? No Robert Schuller and his crystal church?" Shawn asks.

"That didn't happen until after he left here. Want another drink?"

"I'll get it."

"Sit. This one's on me."

Light from the tree reflects along Eric's nose, caught in

shining perspiration. Perhaps his own nose will one day swell and redden, Shawn thinks.

No, not if he doesn't drink as much.

"No girl?" his father asks, on his way to the kitchen.

"She had to go to her place."

"Didn't William say you could bring someone?"

"I thought she should stay home, that's all." Shawn sits framed in a slant of light coming from the kitchen. He shifts his weight on the couch. His face is hot. When Eric hands him his glass he holds it up to his cheek, then follows the ice turning through the orange, green and red lights on the tree. He swings his glass to his mouth in a quick twist of his wrist and catches an ice cube to suck.

"What about Lesley," he asks. "Her room preserved too?" He watches his pebbly ice spin.

"No."

"No posters on the wall?"

"We use that room for storage."

"What about her stuff?"

"Threw it out."

Lesley came home only once after leaving. When she came to collect the rest of her clothes Eric was drunk, as he was most Saturday afternoons, and he told her to stay out of his house.

Her second year of university had been so different from her first. She never stayed home, never studied. They never understood her obsessions or her urgency.

She spent the weekend before final exams occupying the president's office in the new administration building, with 50 other sandal-footed protesters. Eric watched it all on television, pushing back his recliner rocker with its massage unit and heating coils. He watched, plucking at his bottom lip, as jubilant students flung computer cards from third-storey windows and applauded as they showered down like confetti onto the cheering students below.

RCMP officers dragged out the occupiers by their legs and

hair. TV cameras panned ransacked offices. They drew close-ups of dumped files, damaged computer banks, empty wine bottles. Commentators hinted at drug use and sex.

"Oh no," Shawn had said, sprawled on the carpet in front of the television set. "Not drug use and sex."

When Eric slapped her while posting bail, Lesley moved out.

Shawn had listened to the fight from his room, which was next to his sister's, that Saturday afternoon when she returned for her clothes. He heard his father's slurred voice and Lesley's hysterics. Her friends had brainwashed her, Eric said. The university would expel her. Shawn attended that same university now. It sounded as if it had been a better place back then.

Once again Lesley left. But without her clothes and for the last time. She shouted that she lived among the communes on Fourth Avenue, up from the nudists' beach. That she got stoned on hash while watching her laundry spin. That she went home to bed one night with some guy who'd come in, dropped his jeans and washed them along with a denim jacket that had an American flag on the back. Shawn believed her then and he believed her now. He had known it to be true because of the change in her, because he could hear her voice, clear and certain in the laundromat. He could hear it bend as it had bent to him so often when they were alone in this house. He could easily imagine his sister talking to someone who owned but one pair of jeans and a denim jacket.

"Why'd you leave the States?" she'd ask.

"It's the fuckin' war, man." Probably he was from Ontario.

She might still live on Fourth Avenue, in one of the chopped communes, divided into separate apartments and housekeeping rooms.

Shawn studies his father's face. Eric's new teeth give him an embarrassed, perpetual half-smile. This from a man who almost never laughs. New teeth, a first, seemed to soften his features, lighten the threatening weight of his head. But soon his bloated face conquered these subtle changes. His crumbling cynicism returned, and the quarter-inch of excess dentureware became a leer.

"What do you think, Dad? Does William's Christian humanism allow him to love sister Lesley too?"

"She'll need more than William."

"Suppose she'll get it?"

Never meet their parents, Shawn had once declared. You see too much. The father they can't fully leave, the deferential girls they yearn to remain, because Daddy is oh-so-stable-and-strong. In the father you witness what they want in a husband. Security, defeat, resentment. But she will never resent her father for the restraints he places on her freedom as much as she will resent her husband for daring her to rebel against them.

Lesley had hung an old *Casablanca* poster in her bedroom. Bogart's sad watery eyes and Ingrid Bergman, more than one man's lover but still untouched somehow.

Bogart and Bergman. Paul Henreid. And Shawn's sister sleeping beneath their futile love triangle. Lesley did not dream that she was Ingrid Bergman—Ilsa Lund—with a choice of two men. Loved by Rick, saloon owner and gun-runner; or by Victor Laszlo, hero of the underground and resistance. She dreamed she was Bogart. Rick in a white suit—"I stick my neck out for no-one."

Shawn also had a *Casablanca* poster in his room. A Christmas present from Lesley. He imagined her as the available Ilsa Lund when she came to him late at night, her voice bending to him in the black and white shadows, his fear of a revolving spotlight choking off the breath in his throat.

Shawn waves his glass in the air to capture Eric's attention, to draw his eyes away from the tree. "Odd, isn't it," he says, "that an old-time movie poster should remind people more of the sixties than of the early forties when the film was made? Bogart resurrected. And who's Ilsa's man? Tell me that. Who does she belong to, flitting from man to man and cause to cause?"

"It's a movie. A goddamn movie."

He knew William hadn't been aware of it, surrounded in his room by his fantasies of a purer sport. His mother? He's never been sure. How much did she know? Just how much *didn't* his mother say? But he had often heard Eric stumbling, drunk. Lesley crying. Eric's threats. And he lived also with his own forced forgetfulness the next morning when his sister would refuse to finish breakfast and then vomit the dry scraps she had eaten.

Lesley had phoned him twice since then. He remembered the young intern at the hospital who came hurrying out of the delivery-room.

"Congratulations sir," the intern had said.

"Thanks," Shawn had said, realizing that their last names were still the same. The intern had assumed they were husband and wife. He couldn't tell him that Lesley had no idea who the father was.

She called him a second time so he could escort her to an abortion clinic. When Lesley had stepped weakly from a curtained cubicle, freshly scraped but looking like his older sister again and not someone other men slept with and only other men would ever truly leave, Shawn had turned and walked out.

Eric slides his chair forward from the reclining position and stands. "Think they're finished up there yet?" he asks.

"We'll catch shit for running out," Shawn says.

"Swear too now, I see."

"It's been known to happen."

"Your mother hoped neither of you would drink or swear. I always hoped you'd both drink, curse and carry small firearms."

Eric leads them out to the kitchen where he prepares one more rye and water. The ice cubes on the counter have melted in their trays. Eric plucks them out with his blunt fingertips.

"Cool it off a little, anyway," he says, then adds, "to the Pope," drinking quickly and draining his glass.

The bright kitchen stings Shawn's eyes.

"Ever hear from your sister?" Eric asks.

"You mean Lesley?" Shawn says, rye clenching at his throat. "You can say her name. The world won't end. It hasn't so far."

"She didn't send you a card?" Eric swings one thick arm into his overcoat.

"No. Never."

"I thought she might try and contact you."

"No card."

Eric rinses their glasses in the sink. He places them on the arborite counter, then decides to reach under the sink for the draining board. He sets the glasses on the rubber to dry.

"Let's get up there," Eric says. "Not even your brother can preach this long."

Shawn thrusts his hands into his coat pockets, finds his father's keys.

"You fascist," he says.

Eric turns to look at him, silent.

"We're both bastards."

"Yes we are," his father says, already walking out the door.

Shawn switches off the lights. Their footsteps sound dull and heavy over the saturated earth, the upturned garden bare and needing a protective covering of snow to save it from a hard frost.

The chill air cuts more deeply after the heat of the small house. Light from William's windows outlines the leafless branches of a pear tree, black and cold. Shawn follows, up the narrow stairs to the laneway and across into William's yard. Past his father's dark head Shawn watches as the lights in the children's rooms upstairs go out, one by one.

Anarchy & Other Anarchies

You have been searching a month now for the body of your seven-year-old daughter, Alison. You have nightmares, visions where you discover her corpse beside a large rock or under some brush piled to hide a mutilated body. Always in these visions she has been mutilated. You never see the murderer, or a bear or cougar that might drag the body off as part of the food supply. Just this enormous rock. She's out there somewhere.

"Isn't she with you?"
    "Was she supposed to stop here?"

Notes for your daughter's survival. First mercy. Tribal justice. How do you warn a seven-year-old?

"Isn't she there?"

The man down the street at the park, waiting outside the school, at kids' birthday parties, stalking every maze, trapped under her bed, in her closet, on teeter-totters, swings, in swimming pools—in cars cars cars. The man offering candy...How can you tell her that the man on the bus, along the river, on the sidewalk in front of her own home, perhaps kneeling on the street seeking help for lost pets, that the man anywhere might want to kill her?
    The language and the lures he will use to fool her: he might wear disguises, moustaches, false teeth, a plastic nose, contact lenses, thick glasses, wigs. He might dye his hair, have it styled in his apartment by a hairdresser who will alter his part and colour his hair.
    But you want to protect her, keep her in childhood, for you—for one minute longer if you are to survive.

"She probably stopped at a friend's place on her way home

from school. Did you ask the other kids?"

Each morning at breakfast your ex-wife sprinkles tranquillizers on her cold cereal, like marshmallows. You both don urban interceptors. Suspect the innocent. It's a precaution you take now, brought back together by first-mercy needs. You can't afford the luxury of anything less than eternal vigilance. It's a precaution you take like dressing warm, looking both ways, crossing with the light, chewable vitamins.

"...Closer to home, a seven-year-old girl went missing today and her distraught parents have called in the police. Our reporter visited the missing girl's mother and files this report."

You no longer believe that the man with ice cream is harmless. No men with ice cream on their hands can ever be innocent again.

The cop tells you he's trying to do his job. And he is. You know he is. He has all available manpower on the case...
    "I'm just trying to do my job, sir."
    "So is the killer," you say.

They had him before. It's possible. They've almost always had them before. But they let them go, charging $135 an hour to do it. We want laws until we get caught, you think, and then we don't want them to be laws any more.

"Didn't you pick her up at the school? Wasn't that you?"

There's a man smiling in his car. A man downstairs in the basement, when you are alone and the power goes off. Because there's a man every time the parental power goes off. There's a man.

"The other kids said—"

Because you are a man too, you would like to explain. If she were alive. Her brain unpunctured by a rusty nail. Body lost for months, buried in a shallow mountain grave. Her body dragged and chewed by animals seeking to survive the winter.

"—a man picked her up at school."

For the man in the car, for the voice quivering between honeyman and maniac, you scream at your absent daughter: seven seven seven seven years old. And already vigilant. That is not the park. That is not your yard. Not your swing. Not your monkey bars. Not your car.

Night-time, no-one else home but you, and the man with candy in the car waits. Outside and inside. Waits upstairs and downstairs. Waits while you wait.

"Come with me," beckoned Mr. Ellis, our pseudonymous hangman.

Is there such a thing as a non-innocent child, you ask? Our first mercy must be children, you try to tell them.

"We can't have everyone hunting down their own individual criminal," the officer says. "That would be anarchy."

"Men and women defending murderers above murdered children," you try to explain. "Isn't that anarchy?"

Turn. Scan the room. Watch all the wire baskets fill with papers and forms. Police station lighting, telephones, typewriters, official explanations. Words without souls. Techno-words.

"Wasn't that you?" Terror in her voice. "Wasn't it?"

You stare through the slats of your window blinds at the black night. Quick black strokes between the slats. You stare at "out there."

Was it possible you were working that afternoon? That you were at your desk? Staring at the tools on your drafting-table. Everything aligned: drafting pencils, architect's ruler, set square, T-square. Everything aligned, to devise parallel lines, to justify margins. All the tools you use to order chaos. Calculator, eraser.

"Isn't she with you?"

"Was she supposed to stop here?"

"Isn't she there?"

"She probably stopped at a friend's place on her way home from school. Did you ask the other kids?"

"Didn't you pick her up at the school? Wasn't that you?"

So why wasn't it you?

Police: "Listen, mac. Hanging out in bars won't do it. You won't find him there. Sleazy nightclubs. You're going at it all wrong, buddy. You might flush out a rapist or two. If they don't knife you first.

"But you're not going to catch the guy in some dive. This guy's too cool. He picks them up in parks, sir. In schools, sir. Like your kid. Think. Did your daughter frequent strip joints?"

"My daughter—"

"He hits playgrounds. Probably got a map of them. Tell me, mac, did your kid—"

"My daughter—"

"—hang around pool-halls? Beer parlours? She a regular, was she? At seven? Whoever this guy is, sir, he knows more about kids than you do."

You grab the cop by the throat. Wrench him inside-out of his uniform.

"Hey, hey..."

"He drove a fucking nail through her head." Beat. "She

was seven."

"The parents of several murdered children have organized a support group in an effort to raise community awareness to the growing problem of missing children. A member of our news staff files this report."

The police place surveillance on you. They arrest you outside a schoolyard, in daylight. They pull you from your car, for suspicion. You assume the position. Many positions. You are frisked, hand-cuffed and pushed into a patrol car, teachers, students and volunteer guardians watching. "This is a Block Parent Neighbourhood." Someone places a hand on the top of your head as they force you inside. You are finger-printed. Your coins, keys, wallet, belt and shoelaces confiscated. They lock you in a cell for the night.

Next morning they release you with a warning and a trial date. If you were still a civilian you'd feel intimidated.

The lawyers, judges, criminals—they've all been in court before. Familiar surroundings. Only you don't know where you are. Only you don't know how this works, how this environment functions. The others practise here every day.

"We're attempting to negotiate some sort of deal, sir. These bargaining sessions are very delicate, as you can imagine, sir."
 "I thought you were supposed to arrest these people, not act as their business agents."
 "The main thing is to get him off the streets. Isn't it, sir?"

You trail a suspect from a neighbourhood playground through the early evening streets, across one span of bridge and up into the hills. He has a small boy with him, perhaps eight years old. He's a bit taller than Alison, so he could be eight.

He picked the boy up as he collected empty pop cans in the park after dinner: hot dogs and baked beans, which an autopsy will determine from the boy's stomach contents.

You follow. They'll have to believe you once you catch him. This is your man. You're sure.

Follow him into the mountains. Darkness now. He leaves his car.

Smell the forest, feel it shift. You lived in the east for a year, designing ads, and you had been glad to return west where you could breathe green air. Where it was pure.

Wind plays tricks with your ears, throws voices and shadows. He's talking to the boy, low tones of reassurance. Trails twist. You follow a switchback, a series of forks. You enter a small copse, more densely wooded. Exit. Circle the young trees and lose the man on the mountainside.

"...jesus oh jesus oh jesus...."

An interview in *Maclean's Magazine*:

"Come with me," I used to say to condemned persons, as I beckoned them with my hand. "Come with me. My name is Ellis.

"Now at night when I lie down, I start up with a roar, as victim after victim comes before me. I can see them on the trap, waiting a second before they face their Maker. They haunt me. They taint me and haunt me until I'm nearly crazy with an unearthly fear I am 200 times a murderer. I won't kill another man."—Mr. Ellis, Canada's pseudonymous hangman, retires.

You don't shave, don't wash the dishes piled in your sink. Your ex-wife doesn't dress. You tell no-one of the eight-year-old boy.

"Tonight we bring you an interview with the father of a missing eight-year-old. His son disappeared while collecting pop cans in a neighbourhood playground. The boy's father expresses to our reporter his frustration over the inability of the judicial system to keep convicted sex offenders behind bars."

"What exactly have the police told you?"

Your ex-wife has been hospitalized.

"Recently a number of small children have gone missing in the area. Police have discovered a number of bodies but few clues as to the killer's identity. Last night, the father of one of the missing children, a member of a support group formed to raise community awareness, appeared before city council. We have this report."

"The next time some lawyer gets one of these guys out of jail. If some judge lets one of these bastards free. I'm talking about kids here. Set the guy free in their neighbourhood. Rent the bastard a room in their basement. Let him buy their kids ice cream. These bastards spill more for breakfast than most of us make in a year—"

"Please, sir? please. If you would stick to the specific details of the motion before this committee."

You drive from playground to playground.

Coins, keys, wallet, belt and shoelaces.

By night you prowl the parks.
"Sir? Would you step out of the car, please?"
"Given a choice of anarchies," you say.
"We're not offering you a choice. We're not holding a sale."

"I have all available manpower on the case." There is a photograph on his desk of his wife and three children.
"They told me the last best suspect was out on mandatory supervision."

"As I explained to you, once having served a portion of the sentence, with good behaviour, release back into the community is possible after—"

"Just tell me his name."

"You know I can't do that."

"His name."

"Listen, mac—"

"Show me a picture."

"You want to call your lawyer now?"

The gun you now carry belongs to your father-in-law. He said nothing when you visited unannounced. Said nothing when you stole it.

You wait under a tree. Away from streetlights. You do this night after night. You have paid no bills. Your work is spread across your drafting-table where you left it, tools aligned: drafting pencils, architect's ruler, set square, T-square, calculator, eraser. A man steps into light and leads a child into a rental car. You follow over a bridge into a forest until the road ends. Trails spiral into a cathedral of trees towering overhead. His voice as he speaks to the child is reassuring, a murmur you trail down a gulley, across a low creek plagued with mosquitoes and no-see-ums. You climb a rise, scale a bluff and a low rock face, momentarily above the timberline. Then down to negotiate a crevasse you're surprised the kid can handle, but he's in a trance now, fear an anesthetic. Mind not mature enough to believe the terror he senses, carried up a steep incline.

You descend into thicker woods. Low branches and underbrush slow your progress. He seems to clear a path, bushwacking like he's done this before. Your forearms and unshaven face are slashed by the invisible scrub and prickly burdock. In the occasional moonlight you sight his burly hulk, looming over the child he leads deeper into dense thickets, into an open meadow you skirt, a grove of red cedar and on into the watershed where access is prohibited.

You brush your arms and the back of your neck for ticks.

The whiff of skunk cabbage suggests decay. The sunless forest floor slick with decomposing wood sorrel, swordfern, hemlock needles, damp mosses, mushroom spore. The forest rotting beneath your feet. A compost of soil, insects, grubs.

No birds. *That* noise perhaps a marmot, not quite extinct yet. You try to think of the names of more things around you. You used to know.

They stand still in a small clearing near a large rock, a pile of brush ready. He carries a small hatchet.

You tell the child to run, your voice surprisingly cool, but your hands heavy.

Don't look at his eyes.

He smiles. What threat could you be? Out here where he thrives?

He watches.

You think of your own eyes. Tell yourself you don't care if he's never been afraid of anything before in his life. That he should look into your eyes. That he should be afraid of what he sees there. But you can't say this.

The axe seems so natural in his fist.

Run.

You're sure he thinks you can't do it.

Is he still smiling? You want him to rot there. Can he see the gun in your hand in the darkness?

"I've been warning you guys for years." That's his voice you hear, holding you. "The only reason ten people got killed's because I only got ten bullets."

If he looks in your eyes you must be a bigger death than he is.

You don't need to do it, you think. You could take him in.

He takes one step, humming.

You want him to die once a day for the rest of eternity. Starting with today. If it weren't so dark, you think as you squeeze the trigger six times, you could probably witness the surprise on his face as he falls beside the enormous rock.

You shave. Do a laundry. Wash your dishes. Shower and clean, shower and clean, hot water scalding your bitten skin. Nausea and sweats. You left the child in a hospital parking-lot.

There is a man smiling in his car. In your mind he sticks multi-coloured pins onto a map of municipal parks. He is there when the power goes off. For the man in the dark with candy, voice quivering between honeyman and maniac, you are the man in the park.

Love & Limerence

"No more women," my daughter commands. "Especially young ones. My mother says you know too many younger women." She's sitting at my small kitchen table, filling in a crossword puzzle.

What her mother means is women younger than she is. "What does your mother know about my women?" I ask.

Julie woke me this morning with the usual banging of cupboard doors as she made herself breakfast. The longer I attempt to sleep in, the longer and more frequent are the slamming of doors and the clattering of dishes in the sink.

"Did I wake you?" Julie will say.

"No. I had to get up and nail all the cupboard doors shut anyway."

"I'd assumed my mother once was one," Julie says now. She sounds like an adult. She can do that—change her age without notice. One second you're talking to a child, the next you're negotiating with a 46-year-old politician.

"No, I don't think so.... Nope, she never was," I tell her. This much is true. Her mother and I had been too young to be categorized as anything other than too young. We owe each other that much grace.

"What was she, then?" She asks this without looking at me. She seldom looks at anyone when she speaks these days.

"As a point of disorder," I say, "as with everything else around here, I wasn't aware that I'd known enough women for them to be grouped together. You two spend a lot of time discussing this sort of thing, do you?"

Julie stays with me all summer, and each summer she threatens to move in permanently. I live in a small one-bedroom apartment. She says the living-room couch is fine for her.

"Mom says you haven't aged. She says you always look the same. She's getting grey hairs and I think her face is caving in." Julie erases a guess that refuses to fit her puzzle. "Do you miss any of them?" she asks.

"Which one?"

"*Any*one..."

I can tell when she's losing patience with me. "You know you can stay if you want. You're old enough to choose. We can move into a two-bedroom. You need a room of your own."

"I have a room of my own," she says. "At home."

Julie is tricky that way, unpredictable. "Some were in love," she says. "A woman knows." She is a woman, some of the time, as mysterious and—it must be said—as cunning, when she wants to be.

"I didn't know you worried so much. Seems to me I've been hearing a lot about boys this summer."

"You haven't." This also is true. "Maybe you could phone one of them up. Tell her you want to see her again."

There are times when I think she really would like to move in but won't until I acquire a steady girlfriend. This isn't so unusual. She's been living with a woman all her life.

We have escaped several women, Julie and I. I meet them while shopping or in bookstores. Sometimes a friend will introduce us at a dinner party. The tennis courts at the community centre are always crowded with women seeking doubles partners. I suppose Julie wonders why I don't actively pursue these women, why I only respond to those who show an interest. The amazing thing is that children still believe in families. Someone must be teaching them this, must believe it's still desirable.

Women have always liked Julie. They take her swimming or shopping. More than one ex-girlfriend has called from a shopping-mall to surrender.

"She wins," one said. A woman I liked. "Come and get us." Julie tends to ricochet all over a shopping-mall. She wants to know everything about what's for sale: how much does it cost, what's it made of, will it shrink, who made it, where were their parents from, were they nice people? I took

Julie and the woman out for dinner, listened to the two of them talk about the day's adventures. Their stories seemed to me quite similar to the tales players tell when they replay hockey games in a bar, over a couple of beers. But these two order something with ice cream in it. Women always buy Julie presents on her birthday, clothes usually, things she's seen while shopping.

Julie often has breakfast waiting for me when I get up. She cooks pancakes for herself, then keeps mine warm in the oven. She knows I like to sleep in, that I work late while she sleeps, marking the semester's essays that I don't mark during the day because I'm with her. Maple syrup is too sweet and pancakes are too heavy, first thing in the morning, but I eat them anyway. She gets dressed—something that takes longer in direct proportion to the monthly increase in her age—and I wash the dishes. Days when I have to lecture, she comes with me to the campus. There's always plenty for her to do, although many days she just reads in my office until I'm through.

Julie's softball team hasn't won a game all season. She takes the losses well and even seems to be enjoying the game this year. Perhaps this is because she is the pitcher, instead of abandoned out in right field, where nobody hits the ball.

Most of the coaches are mothers and Julie's coach seems to know what she's doing. Her own daughter is the catcher. Whenever I attend a game, and I get to most, Julie's coach lets me handle first base. Probably because Julie told her I used to play. I make everyone steal second. There isn't a catcher in the league who can throw that far with authority.

Tonight's game has the girls rattled. The other team's coach shouts insults from the sidelines, stuff that makes me laugh but which hurts a team of twelve-year-olds who haven't won since last spring.

"This one swings like a rusty gate." It's all old but our girls haven't heard it before. Not when it's meant to be mean. Most of them do swing with a stiff uppercut, but they love the practices and never miss.

"Two-four-six-eight-nine...pitcher looks like Franken-stein." Julie's the pitcher so I call time and walk to the pitching rubber. The girls still call it a mound—they're real players. Their coach has never done this so it attracts attention, a lot of whispering behind gloves. I'm worried that Julie might find this embarrassing. I'm unsure as to whether I should act like her coach or her father.

"This woman getting to you?"

"She thinks we're a bunch of babies."

"No she doesn't."

"Yes she does. I heard her talking behind the backstop last time I struck out."

"Is this Frankenstein stuff bugging you? I could say something to the umpire. Or maybe I should call him the vampire."

"No."

"What we should do is gel your hair and put a streak in it. Get you some six-inch boots and a black suit."

"I'm okay."

"I know. But the longer we talk the more their coach will think we're planning some wild strategy. It'll drive her crazy."

"It's their players that I can't stand. They all growl before they get into the batter's box. Then they stare at me. I can't pitch when I'm laughing."

"I know I never could." I take the ball out of her glove and rub it between my thumbs. The umpire should soon discover that he has some authority to assert and break this up.

"Let's play ball," he calls. "Let's go coach, it'll be dark soon."

"Looks like rain, too," I say, without turning around to face him. Coaches always stand with their backs to the umpire.

Julie smiles, rolling her eyes at the cloudless sky. "He'll

throw you out," she says.

"When I pitched I used to pretend that there was no batter," I tell her. "That there was no-one up there at the plate. I'd turn my back on the batter, ignore him. Check out my fielders. Made it look like I was getting them all in proper position and like I didn't care who was up—they weren't going to hit anyway. I'd concentrate on the ball in my glove, make sure of my grip—I only had one grip. Small hands, right?"

"Right."

"Then I'd look at my catcher, as if there were no batter. I'd focus on the catcher's glove. It didn't matter what the batter was doing because I never saw him. He wasn't even there."

"That probably pissed them off."

She's been testing me a lot with language this summer. Three or four hells, a couple of bloodys, one bastard—her mother's new friend.

"Did anybody ever get a hit?"

"Constantly. You want this ball back now? They're about to guess that I don't know what I'm doing out here."

Julie's coach is separated. Most of the mothers are. We take the team out for pizza after each loss. When her girl goes to bed, she phones me and after Julie has fallen asleep on the couch I drive back across town. The coach calls this "Starring on the post-game show." She buys wine and she brings fresh fruit to her bed.

Sometimes after we make love she talks about her husband. "He really loves Christine," she says.

Her husband drinks, works overtime and falls asleep in bed. No wine and fresh fruit for him. They've been apart for six months. She coaches girl's softball because she wasn't allowed to play when she was younger.

"He'd never come out to watch Christine play," she says. "He definitely wouldn't coach at first base. I conned you into

39

that one."

The bottle of white wine is on the floor beside our empty glasses and the plate of fruit. Apple slices, canteloupe, green grapes. The catcher's mother gets emotional once we're lying together, closer, "pre-game" nervousness gone. She cries while I hold her, until she kisses me, her face hot, damp, lips salty. We make love slowly. She continues to cry, though, clinging hard and urging me with her arms and her thighs. Later she falls asleep. She likes me to wait until she's sleeping before I get dressed again and go home.

I'm not certain if Julie suspects us or not. She might quit softball if she did, but it's not something I know for sure. What I do know is that her coach will take her husband back before too long. He'll show up at one of the games. Maybe even coach first base. That's how I'll know.

Julie has been hinting at moving in for a couple of summers. I wish she would move in, but I know she's not quite ready to leave.

"My mom wouldn't care," she says. "She doesn't care what I do. You're probably stuck with me." She tells me this as she stows her suitcase under the couch.

Her mother doesn't feel secure unless she's part of a couple. She's afraid everyone will think no-one wants her if she's alone for more than a month, that she can't attract a man, that no-one will ever want her again and that everyone knows this.

"She's won't notice I'm gone. Not until the dishes start piling up."

"I've noticed that my dishes are piling up."

"You do your dishes. I'll vacuum. I'll even do laundry. Just no dishes."

Some days I walk a tightrope with Julie. She's not really convinced yet that her mother doesn't want her. I don't see it as being to anyone's benefit to convince her otherwise. After she's made her final decision she'll settle down again, find a place in her patience for her mother.

"So what happens, exactly," Julie asks. "You just stop loving them? Is that what you tell them?" We've stopped at McDonald's for lunch today.

"Would I be of any use to you as a father if I bashed my brains out against this wall?"

A couple of teenagers sit down beside us, listening to a ghetto blaster. I look around for a McDonald's uniform to come and ask them to turn it down.

"I like that song, by the way," Julie says. "You can get it for me if you want to."

"Sounds like bubblegum aerobics music to me. Makes me want to bop up and down and wear lots of pink."

This reminds me of a woman I did like. She played music constantly, heavy on the saxophones. If you think you're in love, here's what you should do: don't read anything, don't listen to music, don't watch any movies, particularly old black-and-white classics such as *Casablanca* or *To Have and Have Not*. Don't drink champagne, don't eat pizza or Chinese food when you're reading, listening to music or watching old movies. Have nothing to do with landscape, sunsets and sunrise. Especially don't walk anywhere together during these times.

Julie's waving her hands in front of my face. "So are you going to tell me what happens? Exactly?"

My turn to make dinner, and I'm chopping green onions for a salad. The lettuce has already been washed and drained.

"Which one would you call if you had a choice?"

I slice two red tomatoes, then quarter them.

"You never slice the lettuce. Why not?"

"Too cruel. Bad attitude lettuce means an altered taste. Lettuce must be torn, separated, gently."

"This makes a difference?"

"To the chef."

41

The first baseman's mother always steps off the bus one
stop early. She needs the extra distance of that one block
before we meet. Even after I know this I still wait at the
designated stop. "Our stop," she calls it, although she's
never descended from a bus to meet me there.

"Maybe if there was a full moon," I tell Julie. She's "shaking well, agite bien" the simple Italian dressing we both
like. Julie likes the dressing more than she likes the salad.

"What's a full moon got to do with anything?"

Oh daughter of mine. Abandon this practical mind of
yours or efficiency will be your future and not happiness.

"Dad? Come back, come back, wherever you are," she
sings.

I grab her around the waist and agite bien both her and
the salad-dressing. "Quick," I say. "Kiss this man before he
turns into a werewolf."

"Women don't believe in werewolves any more."

"Loss or gain?"

"So what was so special about this woman?" The second
baseman's mother is post-coitally talkative.

"Neither of us planned it. We meant to be friends. Coffee, lunch, phone calls on a bad day."

"Romantic."

"Yes, it was." So many people confront romance with
cynicism. "Naïve, too. I took that to be a good sign. It was
nice to think that naïveté was still possible in this
superficially sophisticated society. I thought there were no
virgins or guileless people left."

"There aren't."

"Maybe there should be."

She lights a cigarette. "Virgin, really?"

"Metaphorically."

"Pour me a drink." She hands me her glass. The second
baseman's mother drinks scotch.

"The theory of eternal vigilance has worn me out," I say.

"I'd like to think you don't always have to be on guard, even if you do."

"Naïve, sentimental, stupid."

"Guilty."

She was forever leaving her possessions and accessories in convenience stores. The woman with her music and saxophones. The world is full of corner stores. She left a collapsible umbrella in a Mac's Milk, her purse with all her money and an uncashed cheque in a 7-11. Books she borrowed disappeared into the produce bins of sidewalk fruit stands. Her scarf—worn for show—was left in a Hasty Mart. Leather gloves in a 24-hour gas station groceteria. Me in a pasta bar.

"So what happened to this madonna?" The second baseman's mother sits on the edge of her bed, her flesh now sexless, part of her disguise, part of the façade she lives with.

"She had this Greek girlfriend with an Hawaiian boyfriend. He had a friend. The four of them took a junket to Hawaii. The guy paid her way so I guess she felt she couldn't turn it down. Lifestyles of the rich and famous, right? Pricey way to pick up women."

"Another fantasy explodes. Cherry?"

I smile, stroke her white backbone with my fingertips. Her skinny body, thin shoulders, emaciated chest, sparse buttocks—she's lost more than a husband over the past year, a man she's known for sixteen years. Since he was a boy, actually, and she was a girl.

"She was supposed to be at an aunt's funeral. I can't remember if I broke it off because of the lie or because of the lack of imagination. It was all very upwardly-mobile, all very sunny, very warm and very sleazy."

The second baseman's mother shrugs. "Smart enough to recognize a good deal. You wouldn't go?"

"Too many people aspire to the more insolent aspects of childhood. It must have something to do with trying to stay youthful. Instant gratification, ego-centrism."

"Psychology's not your field, as I recall. Take your 101 textbook and go back to school. Don't skip any classes this time."

"I don't wear T-shirts saying 'Born to Be One-Dimensional and Proud of It.'"

"I already know about you and the coach. Little Christine's mother? Maybe you should wear a clove of garlic around your neck, to protect yourself from all us women."

"She went back to her husband about a month ago. It wasn't unexpected." I don't tell her that the first baseman's mother recently went back to her husband, too.

"And here we are, lover," she says, placing her hand on my thigh. "It's not Hawaii but it'll do for now."

I can't answer that.

"There are no virgins," she says. "Not even you."

"I read about some scientists who say several species of life become extinct every day."

She swings her pale legs off the bed. "Save the whales, save the seals. Do we have any ice?"

School will begin soon, which reminds me of late summer last year. My musical woman joined Julie and me at the beach. Julie went to wade in the salt-water pool while the woman changed in the locker-room.

Julie walked with that heavy dream-struck walk children have when they're in water. "Coming in?" she asked.

I sat on the edge, testing my legs in the cold water. "Nope."

"Coward."

"But warm," I said.

"Here she comes, Dad. She's wearing a bikini." With a small dive Julie disappeared under water and swam away. She likes to do handstands on the bottom of the pool. Her mother has forbidden her to wear a bikini. I'm not sure if that's the reason for her announcement or not.

Later, on a blanket, the woman ran her hands inside my

shirt, one thigh raised between my own pressing thighs. Having abandoned the art of underwater handstands, Julie caught us: "The least you could do is come up for air," she said.

I'd been kissing with one eye open but this hadn't helped. As the woman changed back into street clothes, Julie asked, "Is this it? Is this the one?"

"Could be limerence," I answered, pulling on my socks.

"Which is? And save me from the dictionary." When she was younger, Julie would look up words on her own, but not now.

"You probably wouldn't find this one. It's not well known. Limerence is love too intense to last."

Later, Julie watched TV while I prepared three bowls of ice cream out in the kitchen. The woman unbuttoned my shirt again.

"Julie—" I said.

"She's watching TV."

"What choice does she have?" Julie stared straight ahead at reruns of a sitcom about teenaged girls living in a dorm. "In an hour or two she'll be in bed. Eat your ice cream."

"She can't see."

"She's not looking because she's embarrassed."

Perspiration had soaked through the summer blouse she wore. If we had been alone I would have made love to this woman. The kitchen would have been fine.

"She's a heavy sleeper," I said. "Stay. We can love until tomorrow morning's cartoons."

"That's not possible," she told me, tongue darting into one hyper-sensitive ear, hands tracing figure-eights on my chest and back. "There's a bus in 45 minutes. You can walk me to the stop."

"What about the ones that leave you?" Julie wants to know.

"They've unionized. Demanded benefit packages."

"Don't you miss them?"

"I can only hope that they're deeply depressed."

The shortstop's mother has taken up with a graduate student. She has returned to school and entered into an affair with a 24-year-old scholarship whiz, specializing in plankton and sea algae. She fears her husband got the best of their marriage. Now they are both involved with someone eight years younger than they are.

"It's my turn," she says. She tells me this while crying, the strawberries and whipped cream having done what they could.

"What if I was to cry?" I ask.

"Men don't hurt," she says.

The third baseman's mother is angry because her daughter feels that she would make a better pitcher than Julie. She sleeps a solid sleep, no fear that her daughter might block a hard smash down the line to the hot corner—a drive that could shatter $2500 worth of new dental work. She sleeps as distant as her king-sized bed will allow—"Too hot to cuddle."

The beat of my heart is so strong most nights that it sets the bed shaking. She wakes up, stares at me, expecting earth tremors.

"All the supermarket tabloids predict that the great quake is overdue," she tells me. Apparently, it lurks under the deep Pacific, two shifting plates anxious to collide along the continental shelf. City building codes provide for each new highrise scraping skyward to be earthquake proof. Insurance companies, subsidiaries of the multi-nationals that own, design and construct these towers, refuse, however, to insure them.

The third baseman's mother rolls over again and falls asleep with her back to me.

Our outfielders are positioned there because they cannot catch. Nor can they throw: double jeopardy. Their mothers

46

do not attend practices or games. They carry their gloves, borrowed from older brothers, awkwardly. I gather these girls together in a far corner of the practice field and loft softballs high into the air. They circle underneath, gloves extended, arms stiff, heads tucked down. They don't know whether to giggle or pray. I throw another softball and wait for it to land miraculously in a glove. Everybody cheers, including me. They don't care about catching fly balls or hitting for a high average. They just want to be part of the team.

Julie asks me, "Do you call them on the phone? Is that how you do it?"

I am showing her how to preserve her glove for the winter. We've oiled the leather, which she terms gross, and I've tied a softball in the pocket of her mitt, using an old shoelace.

"In the spring this pocket will be perfectly formed," I tell her. "It will fit your hand as if you were born with it. Line drives, grounders—any ball will zero right in there as if drawn by radar. All you have to do is squeeze. The pocket will do the rest."

The tight frown she gets when she is concentrating on a batter warns me that she is angry.

"It's true," I say, glad to be passing on this baseball lore.

The glove is sealed for the winter and will hibernate in my closet. Spring will be like calving season and the pocket will be reborn.

"If I had to do it I'd do it in person, Julie."

"Call one and tell her you miss her."

"I thought you had declared no more women?" Sometimes I feel we're all just pretending to be adults, that it's as close as we can get. "I'm not looking to go backwards," I tell her.

"Next year I might not play," Julie says. Her voice betrays strain. "We never win."

"Maybe we should find another sport," I say.

She examines the tied and oiled glove. "Something with fewer women," she says.

The woman with the bikini owned a guitar. She only played at being amorous and only when she had an audience. I sang for her once, after we had made love, her white bikini discarded on the carpet.

"In front of the fireplace," she had suggested. Pizza and champagne as appetizers. I could play "Black bird singing in the dead of night, spread your broken wings and learn to fly." She had rubbed her eyes, her worry lines, the tracks across her forehead, and she had reached past the cardboard pizza box, littered with crusts and congealed cheese. She poured herself one drink past her limit. One drink more than she had once needed. As with so many of us, she was feeling alone amid the over-population. What did she want that she didn't have? Or what did someone else have that she didn't, want it or not? I could sense her sorrow, her wine-dulled thinking: "Why can't he always be as beautiful as that song? Why does he ever have to be anything else?"

"I miss the one from last summer," Julie says.

"Maybe you just still think you want a bikini," I say.

"I don't want to live with you or my mom. You're both caught up in the single-parent syndrome."

"Is this fair?"

"Adults always want their kids to be more fair than they are. There's a misuse of power for you."

"Be careful you don't succumb to the broken-home-child-syndrome. You'll be living with that a lot longer than we'll be living with our syndromes. Ask yourself, is this a fight you really want to win?"

"Might as well win one. We haven't won a game since before I was pitcher."

"I miss some of them, okay?"

"Why don't you call?"

Occasionally Julie will regress toward childhood again. "Can I make a tent out of the blankets on the couch," she'll ask. "I could sleep in it at night. It won't cave in." She's never as strong as I think she is or as fragile.

"They need to feel safe, Baby-girl. Everybody wants to take a step back. They're tired." My daughter wants to take a step backwards too, when she's standing on the mound, poised to throw her next pitch, when she's peering past another aggressive batter at the plate. When she's trying to pretend there's no-one there.

"You can stay if you want. You know that, don't you?"

"Isn't there one you could call?"

I'd like to convince her, but don't know how yet, that it will be safe. She can be what she so much wants to be— kind, honest, loving, lovable, an adult but childlike. All the qualities she has watched take a beating.

Labour Day weekend always makes me feel uncomfortable. It tastes and smells of "back-to-school." For my birthday Julie buys me the first can of Classic Coke available at our corner store. She knows my life has been reduced by the corporate betrayal of Coke's new flavour. Yet another blow to loyalty.

"You can drink it," Julie says, "but you have to promise me you'll save the can. Keep it on your desk, okay?"

"I'll feed and water it every day."

"Maybe next year we can take a holiday and go somewhere," Julie says, as she packs her suitcase and the four shopping-bags full of goods she has collected since arriving here two months ago.

"Where to?" I ask. "Just say the word."

"Far," she says, leaving as she does at the end of every summer.

MICHELLE HEINEMANN

Looking for Carey

From my chair by the window, I see the garden. Not all of it, just a small part, because the window is tiny and yellowed. It is like looking at a bouquet of roses and seeing only the one beginning to wilt. Inside, a single lightbulb hangs from the ceiling, casts shadows against the peeling wallpaper. Prairie topsoil is everywhere—a thick film covers the floor and sometimes I write things in it with my big toe. Inside, it is cold. I huddle over my desk, a blanket wrapped over jeans and a lumberjack shirt. It is July and outside it is hot.

Every morning by half-past six, the old man comes to work the garden. He digs and weeds and waters. And when the fruits of his labours are ripe, he harvests. I watch him from my chair, marvel at his concentration. He never shows signs of boredom at work in the cool of the morning. Often I can hear him whistling.

Lately, he's been joined by Carey's wife, Freia. She comes by ten o'clock, stands near him, arms folded across her breasts, and they talk. I can't hear what they say (the sounds of metal slicing into metal, sirens reverberating against the quiet night air, make too much noise) but I imagine it.

"Carey loved the garden," she says. "So often he told me he wished he had more time for it."

"He helped when I needed him to," the old man replies. He fetches a pail from beside the water pump, which sits precisely in the middle of the garden. He fills the pail full of lettuce and peas, garlic chive, rhubarb and some asparagus tips. She takes it and leaves, passing out of my sight.

I can hear her now, in the kitchen below, crashing around. Looking for things she left behind. Jars for pickling, I suppose. With their bent lids and cracked seals. The navy and white-specked canning-pot. Pickle crocks, earth colours, heavy. She will stack her things in piles to one side of the kitchen and later, Vaughn will take them to her.

By eleven or so, the old man gathers up his shovel and hoe and walks toward the house. Obediently, I jump off my chair, descend the stairs two at a time and run to the kitchen to put the kettle on for tea. The old man putters about in the ante-room for a while and when he comes through the kitchen door, I'm sitting at the round oak table, chin in hand, waiting. A pot of tea steeps by my elbow.

He's funny about the tea. "Don't get up, I'll get it," he says, referring to a cup for his tea, and the cream and sugar. He proceeds to open every cupboard looking for a teacup until finally I get up and get him one. The he comes to the table, pours the tea, and while it cools, the search for the cream and sugar begins. I never help with that; I've already put both on the table long before he comes in. Eventually he turns and sees them. "Oh there they are," he mutters, and sits down.

He always starts the conversation, the same list of complaints day after day after day. The weather is either too wet or too dry; politicians and young farmers are always stupid or careless or both; the price of wheat is never high enough.

Today he tells me about Ben and Edward Cummins. "Forced to sell off the homestead. They got too greedy, those two. Always wanted new everything. There's not a thing on that farm wasn't older than six years. And what did it cost them? Their goddamn home!" He's indignant. "Their great-granddad broke that land. Now some American scuzzies own it." He spits into his saucer. "At least Carey had more sense than that!"

Fritz will take this lie to his grave (it has taken Carey to his). I can already see Fritz, deathly frail, reaching deep into his wasted body for one last burst of energy. Suddenly he'll sit straight up in bed, the white hospital gown ripping under one arm from the unexpected strain. He'll sit dead upright, glare hard into Vaughn's eyes and say, "I got that farm from my father, got it from his, got it from his. When he homestead that land, he had nothing. You hear me," he'll scream, "nothing. Don't you be stupid now and lose it." Those will be his last words. He won't even wait for Vaughn's reply. Fritz will just die.

Fritz takes a long look through the north window toward the barn. Soon I cut in. "Vaughn's sensible too—Fritz." My interjection meets only silence. He considers it between mouthfuls of tea. Then next he's at the politicians. I can time the clock by his rants. Twenty-three minutes, precisely. Then he's gone—until the next morning.

I make a salad for lunch with romaine, green onion, baby peas. Fresh from the garden, picked a bit here and there so Fritz won't notice what I took or even that I've been there.

Vaughn and I eat outside in the gazebo. Too many flies otherwise. He's worried. "It's got to rain soon," he says, "or else..." I cut him off. I have not been on this farm long, but already its impending doom is wearing on me.

"Darling, don't worry so. Everything will be fine. You'll see." He's not reassured. I can tell by the way he smiles while screwing up his eyes. His worry is like a cancerous skin. Have I begun to wear it too?

"Fritz came by on his way back to town," he says, between mouthfuls of bread and jam. "He figures I shouldn't buy another grain truck. Says we can fix the old one." Then he mimics Fritz. "Damn foolish to spend the money."

Alarm grips me. The steering and the brakes on the truck are shot. Vaughn promised me he'd get rid of it. "Damn Fritz," I say. "He' not going to be driving it. He's not going to be waiting at home for you, worrying. Vaughn, we decided. You promised me you'd buy a newer one. Your father should stay out of this."

Vaughn sighs and rubs his hands across his face. "If Carey was around, Fritz would leave things alone. He doesn't think I can handle them on my own yet."

If Carey were around, I think to myself, you wouldn't be making any decisions. Carey wasn't big on practical democracy. I don't say it. Instead, I reassure Vaughn again. "You can handle things. You are. Remember that." Then I wink at him from across the table. "Come on—let's go inside for a lie-down." He smiles, gets up, leans across the table to kiss me. We walk to the house holding hands.

In the early afternoon, with Fritz gone, I sit alone in the garden. There is a ritual involved in this. First I change into my purple and yellow bikini and a pair of sandals. Then I smear tanning oil from head to toe, don sunglasses and a straw hat, and with a book under one arm and a pitcher of iced tea and a tall crystal glass in each hand, I head outside and call the dog. "Maaagggieee," I bellow to the east where she keeps cool under a pile of straw in her pen. "Here Maggie, Maggie. Come on girl. Here Maggie." For a moment before she appears, I worry myself thinking she may not come. But she always does.

We sit near the apple tree, full sun blazing. Maggie settles one paw on my lap. I clasp it with my left hand and rub her head with my right. "Maggie, have I got a treat for you," I say. Her ears perk up, she tilts her head a bit to one side and her eyes open wide with anticipation. "I've got a new book for us. It came in the mail this morning." I thrust Timothy Findley's *Not Wanted on the Voyage* under her nose. She sniffs it. "You'll love it Maggie. You'll just love it!"

I begin to read aloud, stopping periodically to quench my thirst. Nearby a woodpecker sharpens his beak on the television aerial. To the west, I can hear Vaughn putting repairs to the combine. I stop reading on page 50 where Mottyl the cat enters the forest unchallenged.

The sun is low by the time I come up from the basement carrying a basket heaped with wet clothes. As I step out onto the front porch, my shadow darkens the warped plywood. To the west, the machinery is lined up against the barn. Vaughn looks robust, innocent, standing to one side of the International grain truck that Fritz bought used from a neighbour in 1943. Stacks of hay bales lie to the north. The hay smell is strong in my nostrils. The fence around the house boasts a fresh coat of white paint. Even the house looks less dilapidated than usual.

As I shift my gaze to the south, I see Freia hanging clothes on the line. She turns her head slightly in my direction, but before I can look away, something in the distance catches my eye. From the junk pile hidden behind the bluff in the southeast field comes a translucent Volkswagen van. Carey is at the wheel. His face is swollen the way it was after the accident and he is grinning from ear to ear. He is dressed like a clown, with a curved rag collar circling his neck. He holds a quinapalus in one hand, which he bobs up and down. It hits his two-pronged jester's cap and makes the bells jingle. He drives right in front of the clothes-line, honking the horn and waving at Freia, but she doesn't see him. Then he heads the junked van to the porch. As he goes by, he turns his swollen head and looks at me dead-on with that silly grin. One arm waves me a kiss, the other thrusts the quinapalus through the not-quite transparent roof of the van. He starts to laugh.

I wake up very early. In a panic. I had that nightmare again. The one where they come to me and say how sorry they are. "It happened fast," they say. "No pain." I vomit all over someone's shoe. Later, I'm standing by Vaughn's coffin, dressed in black, crying. Someone is holding me while the rest look on. But I'm high in a tree too, looking down at the gathering. I can hear them talking about me. "Poor Lila," they say. "Oh poor Lila."

Freia is late coming to the garden today. When I finally notice her there, Fritz is holding her very close. Her shoulders are heaving. She must be crying. "I keep expecting him to come walking through the door," I imagine her saying.

Fritz can't think of what to say for a while. Then he reaches into his pocket for his hanky. "Here," he says, handing it to her, "blow your nose." She leaves without taking anything from the garden.

When Fritz appears for tea I don't get up to find him a cup. As soon as he sits down, I begin. "Jesus Fritz, you really make me mad!" He looks up, rather amused. "You know I don't want Vaughn driving the old grain truck anymore. It's beyond being fixed. It's not safe."

"Well, it could last..." he starts, slowly. I stop him there.

"Damn you Fritz, no, it's not safe anymore. Vaughn promised me he'd replace it. But since you've been at him, he's changed his mind. Why can't you stay out of this? Leave Vaughn to make his own decisions. He'll come to you if he needs your help."

The silence that follows is broken only by Fritz taking long, sloppy slurps of hot tea. When he's done, he pushes himself back from the table and ambles to the door. "Oh, by the way," he says, rolling each word in his mouth as if deep in thought, "don't pick the romaine. The butter lettuce is the best right now." He closes the door behind him. I go back upstairs.

Later, over supper, Vaughn tells me he can't find some new part for the combine. "I know we bought it last spring. Carey must have put it in the wrong place. I've got to find it. We should have replaced that part last summer. In all the confusion, it just got overlooked, I guess," he says. I'm only half listening. Fritz really got under my skin this morning.

Vaughn works past midnight and drops into bed exhausted. Too tired to cuddle. "God damn that Carey," he says. "I wish he hadn't been so careless with that part. If I don't find it tomorrow, I'm going to have to order a new one from Winnipeg. Stupid thing could take over a week to come. Could be big trouble," he mutters. Then he turns his back to me. Throughout the night, he jerks in his sleep. Once, I wake to find him sitting upright, babbling. I shake him gently to bring him out of it and then he helps himself to me.

The clock goes off at five. I reach out to touch him, but he's already gone. Behind the morning call of the birds, I hear the banging of metal against metal. I sleep until ten. When I get up and pass by the window, I see Fritz and Freia talking in the garden. Soon they leave together, headed for the barn. Fritz does not appear for tea.

When Vaughn comes for lunch, there's a lightness in his step that I can't ignore. That, and a lovely smile across his youthful face. I meet him near the gazebo. "Hi love," I say. "Aren't you on top of the world today! What's up—uh—don't tell me. Let me guess. Price of wheat's tripled." We both laugh at the same time.

"Nope, not that. But Freia and Fritz came by to help me look for that combine part. And if Freia didn't find it too." He stops, thinks, then starts again. "She knew Carey pretty well." Pause. "So we went to work—Fritz and me—and we fixed it. Yah, the combine is fixed and ready to roll!"

Vaughn's pretty wound up and eats fast. Between bites, he tells me that Fritz is coming back after lunch. "Oh?" I'm surprised. The old guy rarely returns after lunch. "Why?"

"Fix the truck—help me fix the truck," he answers, then goes on eating. Anger makes my neck tighten. I feel it grab my shoulder-blades, pulling, pulling. Everything's tight. Later, despite Fritz, I sit in the garden reading to Maggie. Once, when I look up, I see Freia taking iced tea into the barn.

"Well, it's about bloody time," Carey hollers from under the truck. "Gotta have sustenance in this life." He doesn't stop work though. Whatever it is he's fixing is tricky and testing his patience. "Vaughn, hand me the five-eighths wrench—this fucking thing is the most useless piece of gar-bage..." and before he finishes the sentence, he sends a piece of metal flying through the air. It misses Freia by mere luck. "Carey, be careful," she screeches at him. "Get out of here," he hollers back. She leaves.

Then he turns on Vaughn. "For fuck sake Vaughn, what the hell you doing. Mining metal for the goddamn thing."

"Can't find the five-eighths," Vaughn manages to reply.

"It's not here." At that, Carey hits his foot to the floor to propel the skateboard he is lying on and comes speeding out from under the front end of the truck.

"Get out of the way," and he pushes Vaughn away from the tool-box. "Of course it's there. You blind, or something?" He curses on for a while before he eventually concedes that Vaughn is right. "Well," he sighs, "guess I'd better go to town and buy one. Jesus H. Christ, just what I need." And before Vaughn can offer an opinion, Carey's off down the gravel road.

It's a clear night. I look up at the blackest sky. Almost too full of stars. I'm walking down the northbound road. Maggie's with me. I feel used and worn-out: flat. It's harvest. We've been descended upon by Vaughn's family. His brothers and their wives and their kids. And Freia too. There would be no having it any other way.

The men are wildly hyper in their nervous enthusiasm. The women too: frayed, running from garden to kitchen to kids. The house is in an uproar all the time. I'm at their mercy. And having trouble staying there. I know about the power of the harvest ritual. I'd read about it in books. Now I feel it in my bones.

Maggie and I walk quite a distance before we head back to the farmyard. As we get close, voices and laughter are in the air. We follow the sound to the gazebo. I find Vaughn, Fritz, Freia, the brothers and their wives. Maggie and I stand at the entrance for a long time and watch.

They're dressed to the nines and are having a cocktail party. When they finally realize we've arrived, they become silent and stand aside for Maggie and me. Maggie is up on her hind legs. Her front paws are in my hands. The yard light directs a beam to the picnic table and we climb it. Crickets chirp a beat. Fritz and the boys strike up the band and we're dancing, dancing, round and round, cheek to cheek. Maggie in a tuxedo. Me in a sexy nightclub number. We dance, round and round, smooth, sensual.... Then through the music comes Carey's laugh. Distant at first, now louder and louder. Carey comes out of the black night driving a translucent scarlet cow. No clothes. When he is so close that I can almost touch him, he scoops Maggie and me up and the three of us ride the cow over the moon. Carey's laugh keeps echoing.

The party breaks up by midnight. I plead a moment of privacy. "I'll be along love," I tell Vaughn, "but don't wait up." Maggie and I walk again—through cut out fields, around bluffs, down silty roads. My senses are so heightened here. The air, sweetly moist. The quietest quiet. The seeing of stars skimming along the lost horizon line. All enjoyed only according to ritual. It is a ritual I never knew.

I walk Maggie to her pen. Silently she takes her place. I walk on toward the house, but turn back when I realize I'm too weary of the whole damn thing to even see Vaughn right now. I sleep in Maggie's pen, warm in the hay.

The earliest hint of dawn wakes the birds and they begin to sing—hundreds of them. I stir and find Maggie nearby. Everything is so still. I walk to the house, go inside and climb the stairs to our bedroom. I want to snuggle next to Vaughn, touch him, be reassured.

A pinkish hue from the sunrise washes over the room. I stop in the doorway to admire the effect. They are there, sleeping naked and close, covers thrown awry. I'm not prepared for this at all. One of me stays in the doorway watching the other of me move to the bedside. Freia opens her eyes and smiles up at me. "What are you doing in my bed," I watch myself say to her.

"Looking for Carey," she says. "We were looking for Carey."

Home Pictures

"Don't admit the truth. Put the past behind," my mother says when we move from our home to a new city. "Start again." How do you put the truth behind you—start again? That's a lie that's a lie. When the lie becomes the truth then the truth is never the truth it's a lie. Does that make all the lies the truth? The truth cannot be altered. It stays with you always.

My father controls so skillfully from his private hiding place. And then he goes to church for his repentance. Prays and prays (I swear this is the truth the whole truth and nothing but the truth so help me God). Puts his hand on the Bible and swears. He goes to church, lies to be saved from the lies. If he told the truth he would have to go to hell. The truth cannot be altered. It stays with you always.

My sister Gloria keeps the truth of the lie locked away in her heart. Her east me west. It's been fifteen years since we last lied together under the same roof. Each year a Christmas card arrives from her never a note no news. This year, she sends a picture too. A three-by-two-inch colour snapshot. She is lying (down) in the photo spread out on a grey floor against grey walls (the picture is in colour I swear) lying lying down. The lie is that there is no lie, the lie becomes the truth.

I swear this is true: the picture is in colour. It just looks black-and-white. It startled me at first and then it gathered in all my attention. She is dressed in black: skirt sweater blouse earrings belt shoes lying black-and-white against her body. Even her fingernails. I get out my nail-polish and paint them over. Burgundy.

I look at the picture all day. On and off. Sometimes I put her on my desk in full view of my work. Sometimes I swing my face to the right and look at her lying flat flat out lying. I stare. She is in black-and-white (though the picture is in colour) so I paint her fingernails. Orange. The lie is that there is no lie the lie becomes the truth.

I haven't seen my sister in eight years. Since our grandmother's funeral. This is true: every year Gloria sends a Christmas card no note no news. The no note no news with her Christmas card this year didn't read "Did anybody tell you yet through the family grapevine? I'm coming home in the spring. My obligatory eight-year visit."

No, no-one had not passed the not message about your visit. So does that mean you're coming? Or does that mean you're not?

At my grandmother's funeral Gloria comes over to me, hugs me her arms quickly around my shoulders everyone sees us hugging the lie gets stronger goes round and round the circle from one liar to the next. The tissue she holds in one hand dabs at her eyes (and comes away black). It is as close as we ever get we stay apart all weekend then go home. Her east me west (I swear to tell the truth the whole truth and nothing but the truth so help me God).

The truth is that we've been apart the lie is that we want to be together. If the truth is really the lie does that make the lie the truth? (I need my sister and she needs me.) Should I see her in the spring? Go east come west. I should go home in the spring. Yes, I should. The lie is that we have been apart the truth is that we want to be together. Should I not see her in the spring? Go east come west. I should not go home in the spring. Yes, I should not.

Which of these is true? You pick. The other can be the lie.

My father. My father goes to church the father goes to church the father goes to church the father goes to church. Sometimes he is an usher there. He walks from pew to pew with the collection-dish silver outside red velvet inside. Gloria and I and my mother sit at the front in the second row and they all see us (the lie the whole lie and nothing but the lie so help me God). Please help me God. I can't tell the truth from the lie. At communion the bread on my father's tongue reverberates, absolving him from the truth, the lie. He is absolved from the lie. The bread the body of Christ and word of the word: my word my lie the lie. It's all the truth. The wine the blood of Christ the blood of those who came before us who lied and lied and lied. He sips and swallows, his head spinning with absolution (the words). Does God know the truth from the lies? If God forgives the father, does that mean the lies become the truth?

This is true, I swear. In the spring, I watch the flowers I planted grow out of the ground. I have flowers everywhere on my land (this is true I swear to tell the truth the whole truth and nothing but the truth so help me God). Miles. Crocus tulips daffodils iris lilies. And weeds too. I cannot lie (I lie). I have these flowers because they seem to speak the truth to me (my lie). The truth cannot be altered. It stays with you always.

I put my faith in nature. My mother puts her faith in lies. My sister puts her faith in distance. My father puts his faith in God.

My father goes to church. My mother speaks the lies. My sister carries the fear. I write it all down. I am the bad one.

I give this story to my mother. She will give it to her mother, then her sister, saying, "She's so talented. But honestly, I don't know where she gets her ideas from. It must be her imagination."

I give this story to my sister. She will read it and then she will burn it. She will burn the truth (my lie) because she is afraid of it. In truth, she will be envious. She wanted to be the one chosen to speak the truth. There will be no more Christmas cards from her. There will be no more messages no more news. Is the black not black? I paint her lips. Red. Should she be envious?

I give this story to my father. He will say to me, "Why don't you write something worth reading. You can write a good story if you try. This one doesn't make sense. Don't they teach you anything in that writing class you're taking." He will give it back to me and tell me to bring it back (to him) when I get it right.

I send Gloria this picture: I am in the foreground. In the background are crocus tulips daffodils iris weeds and miles and miles. My picture is in colour. I swear. My father is colour-blind. If my picture were a black-and-white, would that mean the flowers couldn't be as beautiful?

This is the story I will write all my life: the truth is not as ugly as all the lies. What do you think?

The Blue Jacket

At the party: my red dress, the pink flamingo, the blue jacket I'd found for him at the theatre rummage sale.

The fabric is the expensive suiting kind, creamy light with many thin blue lines running vertically and fat gold bars at unmeasured intervals running the same way. "Here, look at this," I called to him across the rows of costume racks at the sale. By the time he'd found me, I'd taken the jacket from its hanger and was touching it all over, pulling it between my hands to test the strength of the fabric, turning it inside out to do the same to the gold acetate lining and that's how he first saw it. A too-metallic, too-shiny gold with a blue collar and cuffs.

"Blind me, never!", he teased, and covered his eyes with his right arm. (He liked to tease me, call me his squirt-lover, walk in the street gutter with me up on the curb. "To see eye to eye for once.")

I turned the jacket right side in, quickly, so he wouldn't have too much time to not like it. Then I held my breath. Chance clothes like this hardly ever fit him. But the blue jacket fitted. It fitted him in the shoulders so well I gasped. I was afraid to let my eyes wander to his wrists, but I did let them, and when they got there, I saw only a hint of wrist bone showing at the edge of each sleeve. Then he turned around. The back was just a bit too high (no-one would really notice). When he raised his arms up and back no buttons seemed about to pop. I would have paid $100 for this jacket. It was only five.

He liked it too, so when we left the theatre, he wore it and we walked along the street (he in the gutter, me on the curb, to see eye to eye), holding hands. Sometimes the sun would catch his eyes when he smiled. "Now we can get dressed up and have a party," he suddenly said, and before I decided whether he was just teasing, the first details fell from my mouth. "Yes," squealing, "oh yes, with freshly

65

made popcorn (he liked it very salty and I didn't. It always meant two bowls). And loud music for dancing and lots of room for dancing." By then we were passing through downtown and when I looked up to him for confirmation, I saw instead too many of him (of him, of him, of him, of him) in the mirrored highrises. He looked as thin as one of the blue threads in his jacket and so high I thought he might fall over. My reflection, low and blocky, cut his at the knees. It looked like he had stump-calves.

The flamingo was brand new. He bought it at the local hardware store the next day without warning and when I came home later, it was standing in the fig-tree pot in the living-room. The flamingo was pink (of course) and black at the beak. It stood on a long metal rod, which made it about eye to eye with me. I couldn't get used to it being the same height. I'd never known anyone the same height before, so, sometimes eight times a day, I'd go and stand by it just to see eye to eye. There was a vacant look in its eyes when I left it alone, and its ears perked up when I came into the room.

It bothered me to know there was a sad flamingo alone in our living-room. At first I stayed up later at night sitting by it (reading or giving myself a manicure) until he said, "Please come to bed. It's not like you." So we got to bringing the flamingo to bed with us, stuck it behind the bookshelf above the bed at first. (Later we snuggled it between us in bed, except when we were making love. Then it stood at the foot of the bed covered with our clothes to keep warm. Once we were too passionate and it fell over backwards. We brought it to bed later, put it in the middle.) Before long, we made a bracket to hold it upright on the passenger side of our car (outside of course, even in winter, when I dressed it in an old Persian Lamb, black), and took it on day trips to the country and weekend trips to the mountains and to the beach in the summer (by now it had a pair of sunglasses). There the three of us would spread out under a parasol and I would read new novels aloud while he would feed us slices of apple. And lemonade.

"The flamingo still seems sad," I said. We were lying in bed, he was reading. He put his book down. "It needs water," he said. "It's a bird and it won't be happy without water." After that, we always took the flamingo into the bath with us, attached it to the towel rack on the wall over the bathtub. I'd put the plug in after he'd adjust the water and then he'd turn on the shower and soap down under it while I sat in the collecting pool of water coming off his body and did the same. He'd bend over to wash my back, kneel and then bend at the waist, and I always thanked him profusely because I loved to have my back scrubbed. I washed his feet and ankles. We always wiped the flamingo clean with a wet, soapy cloth too, making sure to clean carefully behind its ears.

I already had my red dress, more like a slip really, with its bra-bodice shapely and fine and its shiny skirt with such a deep ruffle around the bottom. I could be gay (in my twenties) then and wear long strands of black beads and black silks and spiky black heels (two feet high) and if I was lucky and he wore absolutely flat shoes, I could look straight across to his chest and come close (not eye to eye, but it was the best I could do), unbutton his shirt, and lick his nipples without him or I moving or bending in contortions to find each other. But I could never do this for long. My feet would start to hurt stuffed in the pumps and I'd have to take them off. Then the most I could do was rest my nose in his belly button. Other times I wore only my red dress, no shoes, nothing, and if it was especially hot outside, I would fix a blanket under the tree away from the street and sit with my legs spread wide to get air. And read letters out loud to the flamingo, posted nearby (wearing sunglasses and the blue jacket).

And if he was around he often came over and seeing the flamingo in his blue jacket, always got excited. Then his sex would charge up so he would need to take his pants off and he put his head in my lap (how's that for eye to eye!) and listen to me read letters too. Later, when I took my clothes off with him, we put the flamingo in the kitchen doorway (by the fridge) where it could look on at us laid out on the couch facing the patio windows rubbing ourselves into each other.

Such contortions! (We couldn't help it.) The flamingo sighed when we came, fell lightly against the fridge for support and sighed. Later, dancing in the kitchen with my red dress in his arms he caught the sleeve of his blue jacket on a hook. It ripped so rough and jagged that no-one could ever fix it. That made the pink flamingo cry and it cried on my red dress and then there was blood on the floor.

JEAN RYSSTAD

Contiguous

It is six o'clock and Candace is waiting five more minutes just in case Hank comes home. She has the kind of supper in the oven—chicken, potatoes—that she makes when he is home, but she realizes, this second time the kids come in from the yard asking, "Isn't it time to eat yet?" that she forgot to ask Hank if he will be home. What time.

Early this morning, she drove him to the dock. Half asleep, all of them. There were no words spoken. Just the code. Candace catching Hank's eyes and, with her eyes and shoulder, directing him to look at their kids. The two of them, still in pyjamas, each fingering their stain edged blankets, unquestioning. They knew they were driving their father to the boat. She and Hank exchanged a look after he glanced at them. That was all. He got out of the car and they watched as he took his long strides to the ramp.

It is June. Hank and Candace have talked about this fishing season less than usual, less than last year, less than the year before. They both know the possibilities. There is not much to be said. It could be a good season or a bad season or a fair season. If it is a poor season, Hank will have to figure out what to do in the winter to pay the bills. UIC will not begin to cover them. Recently, they bought a house, and the mortgage on Hank's boat is always there. A constant.

Their house is an old one, one of the oldest in town and is very much like the separate childhood houses that they both grew up in. The house makes them feel, sometimes, that they are home, free, on a course that has been set. Automatic pilot, as when the men take wheel turns, when they are travelling to the fishing grounds, running all night, at the same speed. All they have to do is check occasionally, pay a little attention that they are on course.

Candace half expects to hear Hank's voice, "Hallo You," at the front door at any minute. She half anticipates him throwing his cap on the table like a skipped stone, the sideways, easy toss, the wipe of this hand across his forehead. He will have a drink and a smoke and take it to the can and she will start to set the table. But, she half expects the phone to ring, Hank saying that he will not be home. And yet, she thinks, it's good, in a way. It means she is accepting, after ten years of this life as a fisherman's wife, that he does not know or notice time. It is a different kind of time. Working until you are finished.

Just as the kids come in again, hungry, hot, flushed, asking, "When's supper?", the phone rings and she says into the phone, "Now, supper's now." She hears Hanks voice and she has to shake her head to clear the channels. He will be home in a bit, he says. He is giving Willis a hand.

Willis has just invested $50,000 in crab traps and has rented storage sheds at the dock for the traps until salmon fishing is over. Hank is helping him move the traps into the sheds. Carson White is there too, and they are going to go and have a drink on Carson's boat after they finish. "Carson's one of the few who makes good on crab," Hank says. He doesn't say that he wants to hear what Carson has to say for himself, to think about it for himself but Candace knows that is what he wants to do. She does not feel annoyed or hurt as she might have a few years ago, when she was just getting used to being alone, setting her own course.

When Hank and Candace first met, Hank would have said, from the phone at the dock, "Grab a cab. Come on down." Candace would have sat in the galley with them after Hank met her at the top of the dock and paid the driver. Later, she and Hank would have gone for the last set at the Surf Club.

She helps the kids get washed, seated and fixes their plates. Thinks of how she might call a sitter now and join them. She might. It is possible to do that, but he has not asked her to. She has a reserve of things to do now that please her. A separate sanity that carries over year round, growing from something that she worked at only sporadically when she met him first.

Her painting. In this house, the house with all the space, she has a room on the third storey, a glassed in sunporch overlooking the harbour.

She'd taken watercolours with her on one of their first fishing trips together. And one night, the two of them in the wheel house on cushioned swivel stools, he'd shown her how to read the charts. He'd shown her how to cup her hands around the rubber scanning mask. The water flat calm, running down the coast. She'd put a little water in one mug and a little rum in another. A paintbrush and a tube of sepia. She'd put him down quickly on the rag paper, captured his ease, his pleasure at the wheel that night. Hank Olsen, his chair tipped on hind legs, one foot beating the rung as the bow slapped the waves, the other braced on the instrument panel. One hand loose on the wheel. He liked what she'd caught of him and the watercolour hung in the galley all that trip for the crew to see.

Now, as she sits on the step-stool his father made for the kids so they can brush their teeth at the high, pedestal sink, the kids in the tub, she thinks that her painting has improved because she works by feel, instinct, memory.

She doesn't mind his trips away, she thinks, as the kids dump water on themselves and threaten to invade each other's territorial half of the tub with their plastic cups. She sees her son teasing, flicking, snicking the surface with his thumb and index finger at his sister, who laughs and imitates the gesture. "Time to get out," Candace says and though both children complain that they are not ready, they climb out relieved, she thinks, to avoid the tears that would have followed as the game built. They waddle like ducks to their own rooms, happy to go to bed.

Hank wants Candace to stay with the children. Be home with them and for them. He does not take Candace very seriously when she offers to go back to work to help out in the winter time. He asks her what she could do that would be worth disruption to the family. What could she do that would be worth handing their kids over to someone else, into someone else's routine? Candace is relieved that he sees it that way because she cannot imagine going back to work. She likes what her life is and she tells Hank this often.

Now especially, in the new, old house that seems so perfect for them, she goes to her studio whenever she can, as often as she can. She can see the children in the backyard from that room and she yells down from the window that is not painted shut when there is trouble.

Candace goes downstairs when the children are settled. She thinks she has an hour or so before Hank comes home. She took a temporary job, telephone interviews, last month, to counteract some of her guilt about Hank working so hard. Now, she has a chance to make calls, follow-up, without interruption. She gets started immediately, without any sighing or wishing she hadn't taken the job. She thinks this is one of the things marriage and children have done for her: put time into perspective. There is not that much of it. Fishing, the time is endless, without time. Fishing is motion. She used to take two days to rid herself of the hollow feeling when he left. Now it takes her only several hours. She has a sense of her own pace and the kids switch into her rhythm easily. They breathe with her. They accept the canned soup at supper, the brown bread—he likes white-sliced—hunks torn from the loaf, tomatoes, cheddar. When they were first together, his homecoming was always a surprise. She never knew when she would look out from her apartment window and see the boats coming in the harbour, two and three abreast. She would watch then: it seemed to take forever for them to come any closer. She knows now, to the hour, when they will come back in. Wives make calls to the fishing companies, to each other, back and forth all week. News of a load of fish, of nothing, or just a few: known long before the men are home.

Candace works for several hours, talking on the telephone, smoking, drinking coffee as she works. But all the time she is working, she is waiting for him. She is thinking sometimes, between calls, between deciding who to call next, that it has been a long time since they have really talked and that she and he will sit tonight, at least, and talk. She anticipates he will be relaxed, with stories of Willis and Carson. How, probably, Willis didn't hear, really hear, a word Carson had to say. Or if he did, and it made sense, Willis argued that it was wrong. They will have a drink together this harbour night and he will tell her some of the things he has been thinking during the day and during his time away. The things she is familiar with but they haven't talked of for such a long time. How he takes pleasure in men's company, takes pleasure in telling her, she thinks or used to think, what he has understood of men and how they fish. She is going to ask him things like she used to. She will say, "I didn't quite understand that, was he smiling when he said that or did he spit?" Or, he will tell her those details without her having to ask because he knows she likes those details especially. He will tell her something technical about the traps or the live tanks and he will take her pen from her hand and begin to sketch the things he is explaining on her survey work. She will hurry to get a blank piece of paper before he loses the urge to explain it.

It will be that kind of night, she thinks, the kind they need to have. To come together after days of travelling separately. After a few drinks they will start to talk about love, being what it is when you have a few years on it, a few kids, mortgages; how they still love each other. How they both worry sometimes about living too separately.

She will tell him how she walked with the kids a few days ago along the waterfront after supper. That is the hardest time, she'll tell him, after supper and before bedtime, when you are gone, to pass the time. She will tell him how they laid down on the wharf and watched the jellyfish swim.

Expand, contract, expand, contract. Moving that way. Not very fast but moving toward somewhere. She will tell him that she feels like that sometimes, that she expands somehow when he is gone, becomes someone who takes all things in, in order to move at all, to push forward instead of being hollow, dry, waiting. Or no, how will she put it? That she does not know whether she expands or contracts when he is gone or when he is home. She is getting confused. She wants to tell him all this.

But, he does not come and Willis' wife, Lee, phones with the drag of tiredness in her voice, a disappointment that is always there, it seems to Candace. Lee wants to know if Candace has heard from Hank or is Willis there, at their house. Candace tells Lee that Hank phoned at supper to say he would be home soon.

"Well, I'm going to bed," Lee says. "There's no sense waiting up for Willis now. If he's this late, he'll be later." Candace hangs up the phone and starts to put away her telephone survey work. She feels nauseated by the scraps of information she's gleaned over the evening. How she can put these bits together to make a picture of all families. She can picture Lee's fresh-baked cookies for Willis to take on his boat. She can see him throwing them to the seagulls when they are stale.

Candace goes to bed knowing she will not sleep. She picks up several novels from the bookshelf thinking that if one does not draw her in, the other will. She switches from book to book. She cannot decide whether to try to stay awake or whether to try to sleep. The bedside light can be seen from the street and when she hears Hank's voice, the two other voices, feet coming up the front steps, it is too late to turn off the lamp and pretend she is sleeping.

She takes a book and props her pillow, fusses with her hair, listens as they mumble, then laugh. Words, then laughter. Her heart beats both slow and fast, sorry he is not alone, excited for company. She is angry, then glad as she

75

hears him coming upstairs.

"Candace," Hank says softly, as he enters the bedroom. "Candace. Come down and have a drink with us, will you? They're just going to stay for one drink. I want you to be with me." His voice is slurred—thick as she has never heard it slurred, uncontrolled somehow, loose and tight at the same time. This movement. Contracting when he realizes how it sounds: too loose, too stretched, extended, needing and realizing how it sounds is then boisterous, hearty. All slurred and jelly like, feeling for the right approach, for attitude, stance. Trying to stand straight, sit straight on the bed, slipping, losing his position, fumbling for a cigarette.

She is feeling her way in it, this liquid, the pool around them, inching along wondering how to move and finally tells him she will be down in a minute. "I love you," he says in this slurred, funny voice and she cannot answer. She cannot find her voice.

They are sitting, the three men, at the kitchen table with a bottle of rum. Ice-cube tray on the table. The back door open for air. They are sitting with the light on bright and Candace turns the dimmer switch low, without saying a word. Hank looks up, stunned for a moment, to see her. He has forgotten he invited her to come down.

She stands in the back door frame, waiting.

"We should get home," Carson says, nudging Willis. "Hank's old lady looks like she's mad."

"She's not mad," Hank says in a voice that brings tears to Candace's eyes. "Have another drink." He pours himself a drink and tilts the bottle toward the men, setting it down before they have a chance to decide on the offer. "Me," says Candace from the door frame, holding a glass out to Hank.

Hank turns. It is as if he is alone in the room now, appraising her. He grins until his eyes can no longer focus. Candace knows that he cannot remember why he is smiling, suddenly, so hard. "Me," she says to him, holding the glass toward him. He splashes a shot into her glass.

Carson and Willis finish their drinks in one gulp, the ice chinking as it tips toward their lips. There is no mistaking the time to go, the sound of the empty glass set down hard on the table when no-one reaches to refill it. When it is too far to reach the bottle. Neither Carson's empty glass, or Willis' rouse Hank to his host role now. He is sleeping with his chin resting on his cupped hands, his elbows spread wide on the table.

"Lights out," she says to the men as she begins to clear the table. She thinks she might smile but she retracts the expression, hardens her face. "Lights out. Go home."

Hank navigates to the couch: three steps forward, one to the side, inner ear; a balance takes him there.

In the morning the kids wake her. She is not in any motion at all today. She talks to her kids patiently at breakfast, asking what they would like best: cereal? yogurt? toast? She hears him, the water running in the bathroom upstairs. By the time he comes down, her face is puffy. He will have to leave again at noon. There is an hour, two at most, to make the next few days go right at all.

He does not feel well. He feels worse in his stomach and heart than he felt the night before but he cannot name it, start to say it. He feels worse even though he thought he might feel better. It bothers him that he will have to leave in an hour. It bothers him to think that he will have to be bothered about it all week.

They pass each other in the long, narrow kitchen many, many times in that hour or so before he has to leave. Many more times than they need to. Each of them restless, pacing almost, back and forth the length of the house, swerving if they come too close, travelling on a course they hope will come close, as if by accident, swerving, a dive almost, to the centre of a course and sometimes they touch, brush a sleeve. Close, but not really touching. They do not want to leave each other this way, say goodbye this way, only close, but not touching.

Hometown Papers

A month ago I sent a cheque for $16.50, the price for out-of-province subscriptions, to my hometown newspaper, *The Heatherton News*. I worked for that paper in my first year after university. I was curious to see it again. To see if anything about the *News* had changed.

The first paper arrived in this morning's mail.

On the front page, there was a picture, a 1″ x 2″ headshot of a man who looked vaguely familiar. The headline, "Local Man Appointed to Grain Board," overpowered the small photograph and cutline.

It was the kind of layout we used sometimes in the satire issues of the student newspapers.

But, there were no satire issues of the hometown weekly. Every bit of news was read carefully by subscribers, read with a dead seriousness.

Laurence Schaeffer? Why did he look familiar?

I went to check on the kids out the front window that overlooks the harbour. They were sitting on the curbside, running toy cars through a dried-up puddle.

It was that combination, the dried puddle, its fine dust floating up like back roads, and the kids' game, that lifted Larry, Laurence Schaeffer, from the front page.

Suddenly I saw him, waiting at the high school in his cream-and-rose coloured Pontiac. An indulgent, sulky suitor, who knew his determination would eventually lead to success. Larry had a dusty job. He worked at the grain elevator.

The neighbour's car became Larry's car. He was coming up the front steps and all I could do was watch. I didn't open the door for him but there he stood, with his back to me, looking over my life—one or two boats coming in through the pass; my kids, playing—as if their existence had something to do with him.

"My kids," I said. He didn't move. Perhaps he expected

79

my congratulations. Perhaps my unwillingness to welcome him offended. After all, I'd invited all the people in all the little hamlets and villages in a broad circumference from Heatherton to come west. The $16.50 ticket. Did I mean to exclude just him?

"So the harvest is fish here," Larry said.

He'd turned to me. He covered his mouth with a delicate pink hand so that only a wheezing sound escaped. He was still fat, doughy. His belly undulated in a kind of inner laughter.

And then he sat down on the couch by the window. He wasn't offended, he was pleased. His pale face masked his pleasure. No, there wasn't much change in Larry.

"Fishing closed last night," I said. "It's closed."

"Closed? What is closed?" Larry asked. The question lingered.

"Fishing," I said finally. "I'm always so glad to see the boats coming in after an opening."

It is noon at the school at the foot of Robertson Street. Heatherton's streets are tree-lined and in the fall, the maples are glorious. I have Weejun penny loafers and spice-coloured nylons and kick through fallen leaves.

The gutter is heaped with leaves but still the trees are full with crackling colour against the bright blue sky. Yolanda and I walk together. It is the first day of our last year in high school. Grade 13. We think the horizon is made just for us.

Lunch hour, a week later. I am dialling the combination to my locker, 36-10-14, by feel, not by sight. I meet Yolanda at the fountain near the exit. She is muttering about Mr. Stacy's stupid, low-level interpretation of *Catcher In the Rye*.

We push on the iron-barred glass doors and they open. Out. Away from the hand-raised, permission-slip environment. No cafeteria shepherd's pie for us. We have been north along the highway to a resort town. Have worked as waitresses for the summer. Have paid rent. We do not see ourselves quite like other high school girls. We go uptown for lunch.

Larry cleared his throat.

"You remember me then?" he asked.

"I was remembering Yolanda," I said. "How smart she was to see and say things. She was a survivor, Larry." Larry didn't know that Yolanda got pregnant, that she couldn't go to university.

"And me? You remember me?"

"Yes, I remember you," I said. "I was just getting to the first day. The doors just slammed behind us. Yolanda and I are coming out from the school. And now, Larry, you are sitting behind the wheel of your Pontiac. The engine is running. The window on the passenger side is rolled down. I think all four windows are down..."

I could hear Larry breathing. "It's a hard top..." he said.

"Do you girls want a ride?"

Yolanda and I look at each other. We are quite used to being choosy—turning down rides—from being on the hot sandy sidewalks, but this is Heatherton, not summer and we want to get away from the school. Yolanda rolls her brown eyeballs. Larry revs his engine. Yolanda and I laugh and shift our shoulder bags higher as we walk toward Larry's car.

"This could be a good thing," Yolanda whispers.

She gets into the front seat and I get in the back.

"We're going to the Lakeside restaurant," Yolanda says.

We all light cigarettes. It is ten blocks, a stop sign at every block, so that students or people like Larry won't hot-rod down Robertson. A pine-scented cardboard bikini girl, her legs curled seductively under her, dangles on a string from the rear-view mirror. This ride with all the stops and starts keeps her swinging.

"Where are you now," Larry asked.

"Yolanda has a mini skirt, which is mostly cinnamon coloured. It matches her hair. The skirt is printed with green leaves and purple grapes and she wears a purple poor-boy sweater. I'm wearing a brown mini-dress, wide corduroy with brass buttons. You, Larry, are taking sneaky looks at Yolanda's legs as you puff the Player's Plain you smoke and flick the ash into the tray."

"She had long legs," Larry said and sighed. "But bowed. Yours were too short, but shapelier."

This was a Larry I hadn't seen, a man who discriminated. Had fussy tastes and had chosen us somehow. I wanted to say, "We were beautiful. Far beyond your reach, Larry," but I couldn't get those words out. For one thing, it wasn't quite true—here he was in my life again.

"Keep your eyes on the road, Larry," Yolanda says.

Larry angle parks at the Lakeside and he clears his throat. I know he would like to be invited in with us.

"Bye," says Yolanda, slamming the car door. "You can pick us up at quarter to one."

Jimmy and Dimitry, two brothers, own the restaurant. They are black-haired and carry black combs, which they use often.

Dimitry takes a swipe through his hair when he sees us walk in.

He delivers two plates of chips to us every time we come. No charge. We pay for anything else we want. Yolanda works here after school and on Saturdays. Lunch is busy in the Lakeside but Dimitry, the front man, always finds time to squeeze in for a moment.

"So, my darlings. How goes the school today."

"Look at all the scabs on these chips," Yolanda says in reply. "They're disgusting."

Yolanda shoves Dimitry's arm away from the back of her seat and Dimitry winks to a customer who's watching us.

Jimmy looks out from his window hole where he sets up plates of food. "I feel sorry for him," I say to Yolanda.

"Are you kidding? He's a sneak. A slime. At least Dimitry has the guts to proposition me. Jimmy just thinks about it."

"I used to feel sorry for you sometimes," I said to Larry. He looked up at me from his seat on the couch. His smile was the same patient smile.

One day, I invite Larry to join us. He's been picking us up at school for several months. Dropping us at the restaurant, picking us up at quarter to one, delivering us back to school. We know he eats at the dairy counter across the street now. It's handier for him. He used to go farther away.

This day, he comes in with us. We don't talk to him, only around him. I am complaining about math. I'm not going to pass it. Larry shoves a half burger in his mouth, then tries to speak. A glop of green relish falls onto his shirt.

"For God's sake, Larry," Yolanda says. She thrusts a bunch of napkins at him. "Math's *my* specialty, if that's what you're getting so excited about."

Thank God for Yolanda, I think, imagining Larry at our dining-room table, cleared just for him to help me with my math. My mother would bring him tea and pie and he would drop the apple filling on the perfect equations.

Larry had crossed his legs. He sat half-turned from me, giving me an ear but not his eyes. He was pretending indifference to my memories now.

"That day, Larry," I said, "I got out of the car first. I stood waiting for Yolanda but you'd passed her something. A deck of cards."

Larry didn't react.

"What I want to know is," I said, "what I want to know is would you have passed those cards to me if I'd been in the front seat that day?"

No answer from Larry. All I heard was his breathing.

I am waiting for Yolanda. She slams the door of the Pontiac but she's laughing. She leans through Larry's passenger window after she gets out. "Go play with yourself, Larry," Yolanda says. "No-one else ever will."

Larry wheels his car out of the parking-lot. The stones fly.

"I hope he's happy," Yolanda says. "Those were obscene cards. Snakes and Donkeys. God. What an idiot."

After that, we stay around the school for lunches. It's too cold and too snowy to walk uptown. We smoke in the snow-banked back parking-lot after we eat.

I heard the kids arguing over whose turn it was to use the "good" car. "Things usually straighten themselves out," I said to Larry.

I wanted him to know that I knew the difference between a little squabble and real trouble. Larry nodded. He seemed to be waiting. There was something he wanted to hear.

"Winter in a snow belt," I said. I wanted to understand. I wanted Larry to talk. Nothing.

"Winter in a snow belt," I said again. "I'm thinking about winter time when you feel stranded, locked into one small place, snowed in, snowed under. When nothing new or fresh can get to you and you can't get to it. Did you feel like that Larry?"

"It gets pretty stormy," Larry said. He wasn't going to commit himself.

"The snow melts as fast as it falls here," I said. "I like the coast. Rain is better than snow."

"Maybe," said Larry. He was restless. He stood up.

"Well," I said. "Before you go: inland. Does that mean anything to you?"

"Just to you," Larry said. "It meant something for you and your friend Yolanda to get inland. It meant everything

84

to you…"

"And nothing to you?"

"Nothing," Larry said.

He brushed his suit lapels and left.

I ran to the porch, yelled after him: "Where is that car now?" but he'd vanished.

"Bobby's had it for a long time," David said. "It's my turn."

"No, it's my turn," I said. That stopped them. They looked up toward the window, puzzled, then turned back to their play.

Yolanda and I scheme about getting to a dance where three bands are playing. It's inland 50 miles from Heatherton. The snow is piled up on either side of the highways in twelve-foot banks. Neither Yolanda nor I can get a car or find a ride to Ferris. We flag Larry down on Friday noon. Our last hope. He still drives up and down Robertson Street every day. He says he'll take us to the dance.

He picks us up at my house. We've told our parents we're going to a dance at the pavillion in town. We have a mickey of rye, 5 Star, and several cokes. We pour Larry a drink as soon as we leave the lighted bridge out of Heatherton. Larry turns inland. We pour ourselves a drink.

Larry is the happiest I've ever seen him. He wears sport pants, not his usual grey suit pants, and a plaid shirt.

He is at ease driving through this tunnel-like network of roads. He knows a hotel where they don't ask for ID. He says it's on the way. When we get to the hotel, Larry goes in and we follow him. He orders six draught.

"Drop six," Larry says.

The waitress sets down six from a tray of 50. The menu here is not beachy chips and hamburgers but pigs' feet, sauerkraut, ribs.

"I'll have a side of feet," Larry says.

Yolanda and I are both sickened, watching him dig and

pick and chew but we try not to show it.

"Drop six more," Lary says to the waitress.

We're sitting closer to Larry than we ever have before. We are on his time. He is chuckling and wheezing, unreasonably happy, Yolanda and I think and see this thought in each other's eyes.

"Could we get going after this?" Yolanda asks. The demand in her voice is softened.

"There's no hurry," Larry says. "Let's take our time."

"I have to go to the can," I say.

"Me too," says Yolanda.

We pee in the wooden doored stalls and when we come out, we don't bother with the mirror.

"We can get him to the dance and that's all we have to do. We can get a ride home with someone else," Yolanda says. "Anyone else."

"What took you so long," Larry asks when we come out. "Let's dance."

"You sit in front," Yolanda says quickly, a whisper.

And though it's Yolanda's turn, I get in the front seat without a word.

I went to the couch where the *Heatherton News* lay. I looked into Laurence Schaeffer's front-page face.

It had begun to rain and I felt so glad. I propped the paper up, against the couch, so the top edges touched the window.

Larry, you took us for a long ride. You left that little road-side pub, timed it just right as the snow began to fall. It was clear and starry on the way out from Heatherton, for all of us. I see that now. Our expectations shining on the road like headlights.

You drove carefully, in a direction I questioned, though I wasn't sure it was the wrong way.

I hadn't been to Ferris since one time in the jeep with my dad, who wanted to see a man there about a half-ton truck. I mentioned that to you, Larry, in a light way, a friendly way, that I'd been to Ferris with my dad. You knew my dad had been dead for five years. You would have read his obituary in the *Heatherton News.* Reminding you was as close as I could come to an apology, a plea, or excuse. Maybe it helped.

You turned down roads and up them. Some paved and some not. I'll hand that to you. You knew where you were going on those inland roads.

The snow fell. You turned on the wipers and they swished back and forth, back and forth between our asking every few miles, just for something to say, "How far to Ferris now? And now? Are we getting any closer?"

You started to drive faster. Your headlights shone beams into darts of slushy white that hit and hit and hit on the windshield then were wiped out, wiped off, over and over again.

Hypnotic? Magnetic? I don't know what the pull was. I know we all felt it, Larry.

At a farmhouse, all in darkness except for your lights shining on it, you drove into the lane. You said, "Did you know this family? The father killed them all with an axe."

I remembered the *Heatherton News'* coverage of that story. I saw it, read it again, as it came up before my eyes in your car in that dark lane.

You turned the motor off.

The newspaper coverage was gentle, like snow, just touching on what might be said. A two-inch story, at most. No pictures. The names of the dead and how, but not why. Hometown papers never say why.

Larry, you said, "Light me a cigarette," and I did and I passed it to you.

You started the car. It stalled but you tried again. You drove straight into Heatherton then. The lights of the bridge, northern lights, appeared like criss-crossing floods of relief. It was only midnight. You dropped us at my house.

Oh, I liked the way the rain streaked down the window

behind the *News.* I rapped on the window and the kids turned their wet faces up to me. They were happy I'd let them play, get soaked, drive down muddy roads. But they were ready to come in. They started up the sidewalk. I pointed, beyond, to their toys. They went back to collect them.

I wondered, watching them, would this day rise from nowhere for either of them. Rise for no reason, other than a picture in the newspaper—one of those photos a new reporter takes when he or she is still fascinated by the way "normal" life continues in this forever raining town—"Two children playing cars in a puddle"—that might be the caption.

Would such a day rise for either of them? Would the colours of their cars and the feel of the cement curb, the look of it, dry and then wet, come to either of them suddenly?

Nothing is ever washed away. Not even a day like this, so unimportant in the scheme of things. A day that means nothing. "Nothing," as Larry said. Forgotten.

I took the paper from the window, folded and rolled the broadsheet weekly and put it in the old papers' bucket by the fireplace.

Yolanda, wherever you are, we made it.

And Larry, Mr. Grain-Board Schaeffer, you made the news. Legitimate.

Singing in the Dark

Building up the temple
Building up the temple
Building up the temple of the Lord
    Boys won't you help us
    Girls won't you help us
Building up the temple of the Lord

Maggie complains all week. Her ears hurt from the loud singing. Her head aches. Does she have to go to that place every day. "Yes," I say every day, "yes, you do. We're going on a holiday, just you and me. Daddy will be fishing. Nana will keep your brother and we'll go away. But I have to get ready. I need time to do my work."

The Salvation Army Vacation Bible School costs a dollar a day. I saw the ad in the paper and enrolled Maggie. Not just because it was cheap and I needed time. I thought it would be a gentle initiation into the days ahead at the Golddust School of Arts. She will have her nursery play class and I will have my writing class. I could leave her home with Bobby but I think this holiday will help her. She is so painfully shy. I think our experience will be good for her.

I've been shy too, and I think I've outgrown it. Outgrown most of my fears. And am strong enough now—to the point where I can share a retreat with a four-year-old.

In that week before we leave, it seems the weather gets hotter each day. Unusual for the north coast, even in summer. On the last day of the Salvation Army school, I arrive in the car to pick Maggie up. She is standing under the aluminum awning of the building, only partially protected from the glare of the afternoon sun. The cornea of Maggie's eye is scarred and this intense light bothers her. She squints with the good eye, the back of her left hand is raised, resting lightly over the bad eye.

She is so absorbed in watching the children play that she

doesn't see me. The boys' play is rowdy: they push and laugh. Maggie is not interested in the boys. It is the girls she watches. They somersault, "skin-the-cat" on the round steel railing along the cement sidewalk to the hall. The girls turn easily, not caring that their underpants show. I see Maggie wishing and then she looks for me.

"Try," I mouth the word, exaggerate it without sound. She takes hesitating steps toward the rail. I nod and nod. She watches once more how simply the other small girls turn, pauses, then curls her body over the rail. She begins to turn but freezes half-way through. She has no momentum to carry herself over, is hanging upside down. I get out of the car to help her but she lets go before I get there, falls onto the gravel. She won't cry in front of anyone. Only when we're alone.

Two women from the Army knock at our door at supper time asking us to attend the closing concert as a family. I explain that we'll be unable to attend because Hank is going fishing and Maggie and I are leaving on the train in the morning. "Please can we go," Maggie says. "I want to sing the song we practised." And so, I tell the women I'll bring Maggie. Hank, relaxed on the couch with Bobby, is non-committal to the invitation, extended to him once again, but later, when he sees Maggie and me, ready to go out the door, says, "Hold on, we're coming too." He puts Bobby on his shoulders and we walk to the hall. The heat of the day is gone now and we're all relieved to be in this softness, almost mist. Bobby wears a cap and Hank does too.

We sing the song that Maggie's nursery class will sing— it's impossible not to.

But when we get inside the hall, Maggie won't sit with her class. She grips the blond press-board chair, sits rigid between Hank and me, refusing the encouragement pressing in on either side of her. When the song is over, we try to sneak out but one of the women who called at our house rushes to Maggie with a certificate of perfect attendance and lamb ears, glued on a band.

We take the long way home along the waterfront. I want to walk at a pace that imitates how I want to pace myself for the trip but we are all walking in the tempo of the temple song. It is embedded. Maggie puts her lamb ears on and begins to sing.

"Look at her," says Hank, and we laugh. She's really marching now. Her knees lift high. She builds the temple with her fists, plunking one of top of the other, and begins from the bottom when she can't reach any higher.

It sounds to my ears like a blessing on our journey. Amen. It must be done. It is different than Hank's reserved blessing when I first came home with the yellow brochure about Golddust, the green italicized print promising a stimulating retreat into the arts, steeped in the atmosphere of the goldrush past. My blessings on his night travelling are also reserved. It is fear, not for the traveller, but for the self, standing still.

On my mother's last visit to the coast, she said that Maggie's resemblance to me was uncanny. Not just the physical similarity but the temperament too. What about me and you, I asked. Did anyone ever say that about me and you? She wouldn't answer, only smiled with her head bowed slightly. She gave an appreciative little snort when I told her I worried and hoped for it in equal amounts.

Two hundred miles into the day, after my exclusive attention, and stories, waterfalls and treats have lost all novelty, I say, "You can go down the aisle, in this car, and look for another child to play with."

"No, I can't," Maggie says.

"You can but you won't, is what you mean."

We sit in silent misery until a man in a plaid wool jacket gets on the train with a barefoot girl. The little girl's hair, waist length, is a mass of pale yellow curls. "Is she an angel?" Maggie asks. They take the seat in front of us and

Maggie doesn't have to wonder long. The girls begin a game inspired by the angel. She takes a VIA napkin from Maggie's hands and tears off a corner. She twists the tissue until it is a snake-like piece the length of a cigarette. They play like this for half an hour until they each have a large collection. "I'll show you my rollies," the angel says and dumps them in my lap. "They're nicer than hers."

I shuffle the rotty things into an empty styrofoam cup and pass them back to her. "They're beautiful," I say and she goes away.

"Mommy," Maggie asks, "are hers more beautiful than mine?"

I hug her. "Not one bit," I say but saying is not enough. We have to look at each one of hers, to be sure.

"What's wrong with your daughter's eye?" Bill, the hotel manager asks after we have been on the road ten minutes. He turns on the interior light of the truck, then shuts it off.

"It's a long story," I say. I ask about our accommodations and he tells me that the building is on top of a mountain, that it used to be the hospital for the miners. Most of the apartments are filled with miners and loggers. They work shifts and we should try not to be noisy.

We are quiet, leaning into the curves against each other on the winding mountain road that Bill drives at high speed. My nervousness amuses him. "I could drive this road with my eyes shut," he says. I see lights in the distance for the first time on this black night and ask him if the lights are the town. He gears down, "We'll show your daughter the bears," he says. "I'm ninety-nine per cent sure we'll see a momma and her cubs rummaging in the dump if we turn off here. Maggie's head is shaking wildly back and forth. No, no, no, she's telling me with her hair. I'm relieved that I can say, "It's too late now, she's tired."

"It's a form of herpes," Bill says as he unlocks the door to our apartment. "Those lumps on her lids are herpes." We

stand in the middle of the room until the sound of his footsteps on the walkway fades to nothing.

Morning. We unpack. My nose wrinkles at the smell of
the old fridge. I plug it in. After a few minutes, the tubes of
quick silver gurgle, spout, crackle. The first noises make us
jump. "What's herpes?" Maggie asks suddenly.

"Same thing as styes. We call it styes. They go away."

I am happy to be a day early, to be seeing the old town as it
is with its 300 inhabitants before carloads of people like
ourselves—who've come to paint or write, make films or
pots—change the nature of the town.

We like it for a while, being together in this strange place
alone. We walk like pioneers on bleached boardwalks, try
sitting on the backstairs of the fake front theatre, walk the
abandoned cement island where the gas pumps' rounded
heads feel warm, rubbable. But, after half an hour in the
heat, I feel faint. Both overdressed and unprepared. Overdressed in jeans and shirt and unprepared for such empty,
still heat, the kind I used to love to bathe in before having
kids. I am disappointed that I don't like it, am uncomfortable, already looking for a place where we might sit in the
shade. Maggie, I think is overexposed, in her sundress, her
little arms and shoulders beginning to get red.

"My eyes hurt," Maggie says, tugging on my skirt. Her
weight and drag on me make it more necessary and more
difficult to find and get to shade.

"Where are your sunglasses?" I ask. "Don't tell me we
have to walk all the way up the mountain again to get
them?" She looks in her pink purse with the ballet slippers
appliqued on it. The sunglasses aren't there. "Don't ever go
out without them again," I say. "Your eyes are going to get
worse if you don't wear them all the time." The bench by the
post office is the only spot that looks cool but it is too public. "Let's go home," I say. Maggie's face lights up and I
realize she thinks I mean home to where we really live.

I unfold the bed for Maggie and lie down with her until she falls asleep. While she sleeps I get out my stories. Try to decide which one I care about most. Try to decide if that is the best or the worst to start with. And, though I am thankful for the silence that her sleeping brings, the larger silence of this place threatens me. It swells. I light a cigarette and the smoke, I think, must be what is drifting, dancing like, hovering like, like what? I cannot find the expression for what seems like regression, my own confidence, resolve twisting and unravelling so that I feel as small and worried by my dreams as my own sleeping child.

Marnie will babysit, they tell me at the school when we register. I am the only woman who has brought a child too young to participate in the junior programs. They have arranged for a sitter rather than the "creative play" program promised in the brochure. "She lives in the orange house, next door to the museum," a woman at the long table tells me, already moving her attention to the next in line. Maggie and I take the diagonal path across the playing field of the school. "I thought I was going to go to school too," Maggie says. She's disappointed.

"Look," I say, pointing out the distance between the public school and the house that's orange. "It's very close."

The mud in Marnie's yard is baked and cracked. Her face is the same way and she pulls at Maggie to come inside with her like a good girl. Maggie starts to cry.

"I don't like kids who cry," Marnie warns. "I don't like whiners," she says, eyeing Maggie with a scowl. "Nothing makes them kids happy."

"Maggie can endure," I say softly with the first anger I've felt in this place.

"What?" says Marnie.

"She'll be okay," I say loudly so Maggie will hear me. I cannot kiss Maggie goodbye or I will have to pry her hands from my neck. And walking back, across the dry field, I feel her eyes, the heat, and walk with my eyes closed, as fast as I can.

There are only two in the writing workshop. Myself and a fifteen-year-old girl. I cannot think of what to say to her while we wait for the instructor. It seems to me that I might as well go home. Laura says her Grade 10 teacher thought she might learn something here. She didn't have anything else to do this week.

Jackie, the instructor, takes a minute to consider us when she comes into the library. "Right," she says, scratching her red hair that is wonderfully thick and wet. That word cheers me. "So," she says, "let's introduce ourselves, tell a bit about why we're here." God, give me a minute to compose my thoughts, I think. My tone reveals more truth than my words, which make light of the trip.

I am intensely interested in everything Jackie has to say, forget all about Maggie until lunch and then feel sad and guilty. In the afternoon, I read out my story, the one I'm going to work on. They like it, they say, but what happened. "I'd like to know the end," Laura says and Jackie beams. "Well, that's it, isn't it? The story must be solved for the story's sake." She says beginning writers often retreat from the crisis. "What if the characters don't know the answers?" I ask. She says the writer must know.

We work on Laura's piece, shards of glass in a face at Hiroshima. We dig for descriptive, evocative words for an hour. I am excited by this exercise in precision. Stunned to see the paragraph shine, glint as we re-read it.

Midnight. Four days in Golddust over. I have a drink each night at this time. Ice-cubes made in an egg carton...one of Mary Ellen's kitchen hints in a magazine left behind. If I take nothing else home from here that is useful, this in itself is good. Tonight, I am thinking about change. Water to ice. What is lost? What qualities are lost when water changes to ice. Liquid to solid. The question forms. How does water feel when it changes to ice? Does water fight the change to ice? Does one molecule say to the next, come with me.... I'm so sleepy. I think I am hardening, forming.

It is a fight every morning now. Maggie wants to wear her best dress, the red dotted swiss with the sailor collar. She insists on wearing her white anklet socks with the turn-down cuff of lace with her sandals. "I can't wash them properly here," I say. They are filthy from the dirt roads. She doesn't care. She is determined now about what she will wear. She says goodbye to me in the mornings, more satisfied, having won these battles over clothing.

Things are more normal. Maggie hates Marnie. She knows she has to go there. When I come to pick her up, she is always sitting on the lime-green shag rug in front of the TV with her felt pens and her scribbler. A bald man snores on the couch. Wrestling on. I think that Maggie probably does not talk all day.

Midnight again. I am lonely and tongue-tied except in class and on paper. I am re-living or re-learning something about myself. That I'll never be rid of me as long as I live. Every day at coffee time the school organizers pass out social sheets, night-time activities, swims, corn roasts and I am glad Maggie can't read. We went to the museum after class today and saw a huge black bearskin, its yellowed claws hanging from the rafters leading to the cellar where the miners' story is depicted in alcoves. A hard-hat with a light on it, a headlight, slicker hanging and tools propped in the corner made me homesick for my life, my real life, not this museum town. I thought of Hank, who always asks for mending in the last hour that I think is for waiting, reminding and remembering. I am longing for rain. A storm, news of fish, money, one good set.

I did see ghosts today. Felt presences, spirits vastly different from my own. Being up here in the mountains, sur-rounded by fire in the bush is vastly different from the coast. They say the fire is all around us, burning into the lake. We must be above the fire here in our apartment. The sky is lower than us. At home, the sky and earth and water are usually one muted colour. I am comfortable there. I am longing for rain. Longing to be home, unchanged. I don't want to change too much but I feel myself changing. Water to ice. Forming. I want to work. There are all these states to consider. Ice and water. Mother, wife, child. I forgive myself at night for being too intense.

No phones in the apartments for temporary residents. Bill knocks on our door. "Your husband phoned," he says. "He wants you to call him in ten minutes." Bill tells me he does not usually let guests use his personal phone but I can call this once, to arrange a further call. I sit on a chrome chair at the table in his suite. Bill has 25 Q-tips lined up in rows of five on the table. I cannot fathom what this means. Cannot fathom it. I ask Hank to give me 45 minutes and I will call him from the phone booth at the Jack of Clubs Hotel.

Maisie and Arden perform in the town hall at eight. I ask Angelle, one of the girls in the Creative Thinking class that has NO IDEA IS STUPID posted on a sign outside the door, to babysit. Angelle has seen Maggie and me walking the long way down the mountain into town, picking Indian Paintbrush and Fireweed. She asked Maggie, "What's your name?" when she saw us. "I like your dress, Maggie," she called as she ran to catch up with her friends, yelling back, "C'mon down to the swimming-hole."

I feel brave and free tonight. Join a group of women painters at the front table, right centre of the performers. I have a double dark rum. My head is screwed on right. The woman to one side of me is troubled and nervous when I ask how her painting is going. "I work in a bank," she says. "I'm not sure why I'm here. I really don't belong here."

The performers come on stage. The fellow, Arden, is handsome in a cocky sort of way. He struts on with a kilt, almost allowing the audience, who are mostly women, to see whatever he has underneath. The standard jokes. Tongue-twisting pub song he starts out with and we all sing loudly because he threatens he will call on us to sing alone if we do not sing together loudly enough. We all laugh when we slip over "sit and sip." The woman to the right of me who seemed so prim is delighted. She lifts her arms over her head to clap and I see that her hands are thalidomide hands; her clapping makes no sound at all since the palms are curled. The performer in the kilt raises his tankard to her.

"I'd like another drink," she says to me and I get them for us. She says she does seminars in Quesnel on assertiveness training. "Come look at my painting," she says. "It's begin-ning to take shape now."

It is our last night. We dress for dinner at the Ginger Jar. Maggie wishes she had a different dress to wear. Bill has fixed her sunglasses so that no light will get in from the sides. A gauze pad on the inside secured with white adhesive taped over and over, built up along the arm. He used his medic kit.

It is a lovely dining-room. I decided to have a drink—a glass of wine—and ask for apple juice in a wine glass for Maggie. It is a kind of toast to ourselves, our trip. She is bored and I want different company too. "Did you like this holiday," I ask, pressing my lips together to keep from smil-ing. She turns away from me and begins to pick her nose. I tell her to use the napkin. It is thick, a tissuey texture. "It won't fit in my nose hole," she says loudly, and the other diners sniff at us, their noses up. "Unfold it," I tell her.

The food takes a long time and while we wait, Maggie begins to sing as if she were in our dining-room at home, oblivious to her surroundings. "Building up the temple,

building up the temple..." I am embarrassed, not so much
for the singing as the song.

On the way home, before our last climb up the mountain,
we call Hank. "I love you guys," he says. A friend was struck
in the chest when a cable snapped. Like a shot from a gun.
Instant. He would not have known what hit him, Hank
says. They think the skipper might not have followed safety
regulations. Inquest. "It's okay if you've spent all your
money," he says. "Spend more."

Okay if you have an ugly haircut.

Okay if you are lonesome.

I believe him. Maggie and I start the walk back. The
school is all closed down for another year. Over, and I have
just begun.

The sky is peacock blue, not black. And the wind is
strong. "Hold on to my hand or I'll blow away," Maggie
says. There are no street lights. Only lights in a few houses.
The rest are empty airy-looking places. I have not felt this
alert to danger since we came. The fire in the mountain did
not scare me like this whistle through the mountains and
this peacock sky, unreal peacock sky. It is a scream, stream
of air that cannot get out of a tunnel, an owl in a barrel. A
cat takes cover, disappears. Maggie and I are of one accord.
To get home. Enough. Enough for now. We did it, we've
done it. Got through it. Let's go home. We are walking very
quickly. There are pants hanging on a porch on a hanger,
folded over, swinging wildly along the clothes-line. No
lights on in the house. A shed, wood piled inside, the door
agape. Black, black in that hole. I press my lips thinking
this is so stupid to have this much fear. A little change in the
weather. The atmosphere.

Maggie has a fierce expression, her sandalled feet slap on
the hard, worn gravel road. We are holding tight. We have
never walked together in fear before.

"Do you want to sing the temple song?" she says and
starts to sing without me. I join in. We yell the parts about

Boys won't you help us. We are nearly up the mountain now and are laughing at ourselves as the hotel, the old hospital lights shine on the path.

We walk slower, almost leisurely and the wind has died. Strangely, I think, dropped down exhausted.

"Did you ever sing that loud in the dark before?" Maggie asks, her voice full of wonder.

"No," I say. "But my mother used to tell me to sing loud when I was afraid."

"And did anything happen to you?" Maggie asks.

She means in my experience, is it generally safe to sing in the dark. "What do you think?" I ask.

Sixteen hours, all night riding back to the coast. Nothing matters except getting home. She is so tired. I am so tired. But she will not sleep alone in a seat, stretch out. We doze on each other. She likes it best in my arms and I feel so tender toward her. About an hour from home, we eat crackers, cheese, apple juice. She vomits chunks, then liquid over me. My arms, my jeans, my blouse. I get water from the smelly bus toilet, sponge us both off. We joke about things, how rotten we smell, in a soft sort of way, nuzzling. I tell her sweet things about puddles, anything wet, fresh and familiar to her that I can think of and she falls asleep. We are nearly home.